ILLINOIS SHORT FICTION

A list of books in the series appears at the end of this volume.

Nancy Potter

Legacies

UNIVERSITY OF ILLINOIS PRESS

Urbana and Chicago

Publication of this work was supported in part by grants from the Illinois Arts Council, a state agency, and the National Endowment for the Arts.

The author remains grateful to the Corporation of Yaddo, MacDowell Colony, Montalvo Center for the Arts, National Endowment for the Arts, Tyrone Guthrie Centre at Annaghmakerrig, University of Rhode Island, and Virginia Center for the Arts.

This book is printed on acid-free paper.

"The Guests," *Liberal and Fine Arts Review* 2, no. 1 (January 1982)
"A Thin Place," *Bloodroot* 8 (Winter 1981)
"A Short Vacation," *Piedmont Literary Review* (Fall 1986)
"Viewing the Remains," *Indiana Review* 8, no. 2 (Spring 1985)
"Gypsies," *Alaska Quarterly Review* 3, nos. 1 & 2 (Fall/Winter 1984)
"A Private Space," *The Round Table* 1, no. 1 (Fall 1984)
"The Woman Who Would Not Stay Home," *North American Review* 266, no. 2 (June 1981)
"Light Timber," *The Treasury of American Short Stories* (Doubleday, 1981)
"Pen Pals," PEN/NEA Syndicated Fiction Project
"Safe Home," *Kansas Quarterly* 16, nos. 1 & 2 (Winter/Spring 1984)
"Calendar Day," *Nimrod* 26, no. 1 (Fall/Winter 1982)
"The Bigamist," *The Available Press/PEN Short Story Collection* (Ballantine, 1985)
"Talking to Trees," *Blueline* 6, no. 2 (Winter/Spring 1985)

Library of Congress Cataloging-in-Publication Data

Potter, Nancy A. J.
    Legacies.

    (Illinois short fiction)
    I. Title II. Series.
PS3566.07L4   1987   813'.54   86-30851
ISBN 0-252-01428-6 (alk. paper)

For Nancy Sullivan

Contents

Legacies

We are sitting in Carthage, dividing the spoils. My brother, Carl, and I have come from opposite ends of the country to spend a few hours in the ugliest room of the unattractive house in which we grew up, some years apart, in Carthage, Nebraska. Our mother died last week, but, superstitiously, we have to touch this kitchen table before we can be sure.

There is nothing left, but we still have come to claim our inheritance. There is no will, no fortune, no inheritance, no family really. But growing up in this house, we are experts in the rituals of last wishes, estates, wills, and probate. We know all the folklore but none of the matching emotions.

Remember how people used to hope that their ships would come in? Are you in the will? Did she leave you anything? They searched for four-leaf clovers and remembered the shapes of matted tea leaves in the cup. They read the tempting advertisements: Will Martha Tubridy (or Twobirdy) once of the Woodlawn section call Eaton, Sheedy, and Trowbridge. It will be to her advantage. They had heard tell of mysterious benefactors. A shabby man had willed his unsuspected fortune to the waitress who had served him breakfast for thirty years in the Childs on Exchange Street. He did not even know her whole name. She was only "Mildred," in white embroidery on her uniform pocket. And there was the lucky dog, Trixy, living on the income of twenty million before the principal went to psychic research.

What you received finally could be disappointing: a big corroded cross in a crushed jewelry box, a watch chain made of someone's tightly braided hair, a black onyx ring caught in a white-gold basket, the onyx chipped. The rest of your inheritance—the Log Cabin quilt carried west out of Ohio in 1830 and the Saint Louis Exposition souvenir spoons—were supposedly in a wooden trunk in the attic. But when the trunk could be opened, it revealed less satisfactory relics: some rolls of elaborate crochet lace badly stained, a bundle of explicit love letters that weren't even interesting, several large yellow teeth, a bunch of rusty keys to houses that had been sold or burned down, and several studio photographs of babies, no one could remember whose. And some families saved the wrong things, the wrappings rather than the items. So there would be boxes inside of boxes, with neatly folded paper and ribbon in the smallest. So much for treasures.

Some families with perfect recall inventoried the spoils. Who got Uncle Hal's ruby studs? Where did Aunt Maud's cameos go? Where is the stamp collection? She promised me the breakfront and I only got the Wedgewood vase.

I had a friend who spent her life with a sick old uncle, being promised a half million. He outlived her by fifteen years. I was supposed to leave my Burberry coat, which has since worn out, to another friend who gained a hundred pounds and couldn't get her arm into it anyway. Legacies are like lotteries. First you are poor and have nothing anyone else would want, and then one day you may wake up too rich to want anything. You often get what you don't need or just after that need has passed. Sometimes you're grateful to get nothing. Then you don't have to pay the storage.

In Carthage when I grew up making your will was an acceptable form of pure recreation. An exercise in self importance. Even if you had next to nothing, you continually planned its distribution. You made an appointment and climbed to a second-story office on Main Street to see a lawyer you thought you might trust, though, of course, all of them were crooks. The office was brown wood with the look of absorbed misery like church or purgatory. After all the loopholes had been plugged and the distribution of goods assured, you might ask the smart young lawyer, "But how will you know I'm dead?" And he would reply, "No problem. We read the death notices first thing every morning. Then we swing into action." Assured that you might have control of a few minutes into the afterlife, you could confidently go down the stairs and start designing codicils.

But not my mother. Perhaps she did not believe that she would die. Or perhaps she never found a lawyer she could trust enough. Or she did not want to acknowledge my brother and me as heirs. Or she simply had a primitive fear of being captured in some probate ledger. She had subtle ways of outwitting the officials. She changed her first name from Agnes to Lillian and managed to get her birth certificate permanently lost. Being assigned a social security number was indignity enough.

And all those instructions about the funeral that are so often discovered in the will too late, she had shouted repeatedly into the right ears before she gave up speaking: no service, no visiting hours, no flowers, cremated immediately and put into that spot in the upper right corner of the Nelligan lot, the last space left. She threatened me: "I'll haunt you if you don't follow what I want done. I don't want you or anyone else standing around gawking at me in the box."

She knew how to preserve her margins. She was a strong-willed woman and went down slowly, dying from the top down like a reluctant tree. Since I saw her seldom and our communication was never good, the process was mysterious to me. She was disgusted at losing the upper hand. It seemed indecent for me to walk in and out of the room in the nursing home where she was prisoner.

Then she stopped talking entirely. She fixed an angry gaze over my left shoulder. In my monologues with her, there were so many dangerous topics, I felt I was in a mine field. I couldn't mention the home (where she pretended that she wasn't), my failed marriage and lost child, or religion, which had also dropped away. Or my brother, Carl, especially. For years he had been the blankest space in our thin dialogue. And not only for being gay. Once he had been the favorite, her change-of-life baby. In our telephone conversations as he was growing up, she would report nervously, "He's peculiar. He lies in the dark at the bottom of his bed looking, he says, at the stars dancing. Did you ever hear anything more ridiculous? It's as if there's a cloud over him. He's in a fog."

Later she began to delete references to Carl, and, of course, she

spread disappearing powder over the name of his lover, Roy. Carl met
Roy almost fifteen years ago in a VA hospital after Vietnam. Roy has 80
percent disability, stays at home, is a good cook. I only know about
him from their Christmas cards. Carl repairs computers, probably
earns five times what I do.

We are hardly a family at all, I thought, during what turned out to be
my last visit with my mother. She sat in a dark corner of room 10 of
the Hillcrest Manor in her own rocker brought from home, while I
fired half-hearted questions at her. "Want me to put on the lights?
Won't dinner be along soon?" She scowled and made an impatient
gesture as if she wanted to wash her hands of me and dinner.

"All right. I'll leave you alone. I've bothered you enough for today."
She gave no sign of hearing. I ought to touch her, I thought. At least
that. But as I drew close to the chair, I could feel her cowering. My
gesture toward the dignity they're always mouthing in these places was
to clear out without fake cheeriness or blown kisses. I just turned and
scuffed out, feeling brutal.

I had an appointment down the hall with the social worker. The
social worker was fresh out of graduate school, twenty-five years younger than I, but well trained to avoid talking down.

"I have to get down to the basics with you." She spoke directly into
my face and slowly, as if I should read her lips. She was not expecting
response, but giving facts. "Your mother had to sign over the house to
the county. We don't want to bother her with too many papers. As you
know, she is threatened by becoming a welfare patient. So the house is
her line of credit. Look at it as collateral."

"This is what they saved for. She ought to use it all up."

"I'm afraid that there isn't anything left except for the house. We've
put away any papers she had in a secure place—actually, her handbag,
which is in the safe here. You'll have a chance to examine it, but we
simply wanted you to know that your mother will be cared for, no
matter what. We will deduct her share of the bill from the value of
the house."

"Anything that makes her comfortable," I said. "Money was a dangerous topic for us." I thought that this conversation was dangerous
too. "If it comes to that, I suppose you will sell the house."

"At the very end. We hope that it won't come to that. The problem is what has happened to property values, especially in the east end of town." What she meant was that the original city had died entirely. Or it had packed up and moved out to the interstate and nothing was going to entice it back. I was pretty sure that the social worker lived on the up-and-coming west end of town. "Anyway, we don't want her to worry about money. But it seems to be an obsession with her."

"She was an accountant," I said. That's not exactly true, but it was an affectation worthy of her. She kept the books, such as they were, for my father's paper store. She was not especially good at doing anything, but she concealed her limits well. She was neat, which some high school teacher must have associated with bookkeeping. But my father had too little business to justify her help. Besides, he was trying to hide his failures. They were good at hiding failure from each other and from themselves. That is one asset of a big house. You can sometimes hide your misery.

"Your mother has strong ideas. She's made up her mind about many things and we don't want to upset her." The staff must have been having a rough time with her, but I wasn't about to apologize. Long before meeting my father or me or Carl, my mother had made up her mind about her living and her dying.

"She has a right," I said lamely. I knew that I ought to defend her more vigorously, but I was tired and it was too late in the game.

"We respect her wishes." *Respect* and *dignity* were frequent words here.

I felt that the interview had gone badly. "I wish that I lived nearer. It's hard for me to leave my job. And really we haven't been especially close over the years."

"And there's your brother, also far away." I nodded. Carl and Roy live in San Francisco. I live alone in Rhode Island, and my mother was attempting not to outlive her assets in the middle of the country.

"Your mother wouldn't make a will." That didn't surprise me. She had been more secretive than an undercover agent, especially about money. "We encourage patients to make definite plans. It has psychological value for them. And, of course, it makes it much easier for the family." She frowned over the chart. "I notice that she refused the lawyer five times and said that she had no interest in seeing any of our chaplains. Actually, she instructed us to forbid visitors of any kind. Even . . ." she stopped.

"Even family," I finished confidently. "Even my brother or me."

"On the other hand," the young woman said, "you have your rights. The family has rights too."

So you may understand why I didn't kill myself to get back to the Manor quickly. Anyway, it was within the next month that the call came from Hillcrest that my mother had "slipped away" the night before. For several years I have been responsible for the care and health of more than a hundred expensive animals at the city zoo. Mother died during one of the worst blizzards of the century. I was staying night and day in the zoo. Half of the staff couldn't get in, and I was dragging sacks of grain and chopping vegetables and nursing a temperamental monkey with a scary temperature.

It was a whole day and night before I could get back to my apartment to call Carl. I don't like using the city phones for personal calls and, anyway, I wanted to prepare myself. It had been a couple of years since I had talked with him. I had thought that this silence might be for keeps. The words were like brillo pads being pulled out of my throat.

As the telephone bored into the open space of the San Francisco house, I hoped that no one was at home, especially not Roy. But, of course, it was Roy who finally answered. When we were exchanging Christmas cards, Carl had sent me a snapshot of the two of them, standing beside each other in the same living room where Roy had picked up the phone. Carl had shrunk, it seemed. Once fresh faced and elfin, he looked knobby and ravaged. Roy was big, fleshy, seeping out of his clothes. There were the usual hanging plants and big unframed canvases and wicker furniture and windows open, the way we think of California.

"Oh, Elizabeth!" Roy said. "I mean, Beth! Oh, Carl's not here. He works with a support group. Tuesday's his night. I'll give him any message. Or do you want him to give you a call? It'll be late, though."

"No. I have to go to sleep myself now. We've had a blizzard, and I haven't slept for a couple days. I can't get back to sleep if I'm awakened. But you tell him this. Mother died yesterday. There's no service, of course, but I'm going out to Carthage next weekend to take care of

things. I'll be there Saturday afternoon at the house if he can make it. If
not, all right."

"I'm sure that he'll want to be there."

"Well, I'm not so sure. Tell him there's not much to do. He really
doesn't have to come."

"I know he'll want to be with you. I'm awfully sorry. Is there anything I can do?"

What could he do? What could any of us do? We hung up.

We come from modest circumstances. In Carthage the genteel poor,
the shopkeepers, had only their good names—Fine Day Fontaine,
Banjo Babcock, and our own grandfather, Nickel Nelligan. Our first
inheritance, the corner store, was our millstone. Grandfather drank
himself to death before I was aware of the store. That was before I was
born. But when I was growing up in Carthage, what your father did set
the whole pattern of life. The baker's kids got up at three to heat the
ovens and knead the dough. Flour settled in their hair, as manure
stained the farm boys' highcuts.

Mother's father had been an organist, dirt poor and pretentious, and
he ran out on his family, just disappeared with a soprano. When my
mother married into the Nelligan store, she guaranteed our failure.
Any sensible person would never have stepped across the threshold.
The grouchy owner glowered over the cash register, suspecting you of
wasting his time or stealing or upsetting the stock. The gold-leaf sign
said Nelligan's Notions, but my father cut out the notions, boarded up
most of the space, sold only papers and cigarettes and chewing gum.
Then he let the clerk go, which left him standing six to six on his
swollen feet with nothing to look forward to except stacks of unsold
Newsweeks, an almost inedible supper, and another bundle of *Chroni-
cles* thrown against the door by the driver of the 5:45 Greyhound the
next morning.

"I wish that you'd wash your hands," Mother would say.

"I have," he would answer. "Can't you smell the Cashmere Bouquet?"

"They seem stained. They look dirty to me."

Every night at the kitchen table he wrapped the change from the
leather pouch into rolls, which she deposited at the First Trust Company. His hands were gray and greasy. So were mine. I made towers

and bridges and chimneys of the nickels and dimes. "Don't play with the money," she said. My hands wore an acrid smell.

Now you can buy the *Chronicle* or *USA Today* right out of a machine at the corner, in front of the small blank space where Nelligan's was. The First Trust Company has moved into a cinder-block sprawl on Frontage Road, abandoning its Roman temple. Something called Community Action, the major business left downtown, has moved into the old bank building. It was there in one of the cubby-hole offices that I picked up the key to what had been my mother's house and her plastic handbag containing what the supervisor called her "valuables." The county would try to recover most of her hospitalization costs by an auction later, but I was certainly welcome to any small "personal effects" in the house. From their indifference, I got the impression that it would be a favor if I cleaned out the place and torched it. Save them the trouble.

It is February, the quick month, gone before you notice it. Back at the park where I work, under the frozen surface of the pools, the goldfish are slowly opening and shutting their delicate orange mouths. Then the purple finches will come one day to the feeders, and suddenly the redwings are back. None of the other Nelligans liked such country things. I never let on to my mother that I worked at the zoo. I told her it was the recreation department.

Walking into my mother's empty and neglected house, I am terribly uneasy. The heavy air is sour. I push myself to turn on the oven and sit in the small comfort of its open door. Upstairs I find and put on my mother's best coat—an important winter coat, black, of course, and old enough to have fur trim. Although I don't own a fur coat, that's not a moral statement. It's no drain on the wild population to have mink ranches. Besides, these scraps of Persian paw have been around the house as long as I can remember, being taken off one coat and sewn onto another. By now they are domesticated. The coat is long, abundant as a robe, and nearly indestructible. In one pocket are two 1970 quarters and a totally new linen handkerchief, hand edged, the tag says, in Portugal.

Doors slam and there is Carl, suddenly out of a taxi as if he had just come home from school, except, of course, no one ever took a taxi to this house. I advance, tilt my cheek as they do on the soap operas, but he wraps me in his tense arms. He looks brown and healthy, which I resent a little.

"Well here we are. The mansion to ourselves. All the ties that bound got busted, huh? I came by way of the grave. Best part of the cemetery. Full up with the elite from the 1920s. Guaranteed no riffraff, almost no visitors. Just wanted you to know."

"I wasn't checking up. We're not making points now."

Carl squints up at the bare bulb in the center of the kitchen ceiling. "Want to bet? Twenty watts?"

"She could see like a mole. Another small economy."

"And for what? Can you remember one good meal here? Or a happy one? I know that I shouldn't show resentment. After all, I'm alive, and that's the big difference."

"She did her best. She wasn't cut out to be a mother or married, but what could she do?"

"And we weren't cut out to be her children, either." He touches the dusty table. "When I think of loneliness, I think of them sitting here together. That was loneliness."

His memory of our parents is even sharper and more painful than mine. We were each almost like only children, overlapping just a bit. Once home for Thanksgiving from my first job, I came upon him going through my suitcase. He must have been five or six, a tiny, easily threatened child whose white face had almost no expression. He was like an opossum frozen by approaching car lights. I backed out of the room and made a lot of noise coming back in. It seemed like ten minutes later that he was in Vietnam.

"We're orphans now," he says. "I never thought I'd live this long. First you're the youngest person in every room and then one day you wake up and nobody's older."

"We have to settle some things today. We didn't come all this way to talk about mortality."

"Our inheritance. That's what we have to sort out, isn't it?"

I flinch, but he goes right on. "And there's less than nothing to share, I take it. Deep into the minus column. Nothing to be taken away from zero." I have forgotten how dangerous talking with him is, like skating along near open water.

"I'm not playing according to the rules, am I?" he says. "Supposed to keep up a solid front. You know, I was thinking as I drove up that Mom and Dad thought they had no backs."

"What do you mean?"

"They had the front of the house painted. Only the front. Dickied up the porch with petunias and two wicker chairs. Not that anyone sat there. They painted the rotted porch steps every spring. They only looked at themselves from the front."

Carl was late in talking, but when he began, it gushed out, stripping off the varnish like lye. Mother used to say, "He tells everything. I want to put my hands over my ears. I don't want to know anything more. Why does he bother me with such things? I'm too old for all that trouble."

"Well, live and let lie. Be simple. Be glad for health and a round-trip ticket." Carl touches his cigarette pocket.

"It's all right," I say. "Nobody's looking over your shoulder now. Use that vase for an ash tray." I bring it from the window sill. It is painted china, two fat children grinning under an umbrella.

"I never did figure out what she wanted of me," Carl traces the stubby forms on the vase. "To be normal, I suppose. As if they were such great models. Or you, for that matter."

Growing up, I had my eyes set only on freedom. "I like the strange," I kept saying. "I want adventure." That was more hope than truth. I was hungry for love or violence, couldn't tell the difference. I must have scared my husband, who could have been a loving man. I had the one son and lost him. He favored his dad from the start, and after the divorce and my husband's remarrying, he went on living in their house as if I hadn't happened. I was meant to live alone. Some animals are. There is a camel, for instance, at the zoo that gets nervous the minute she sees one of her kind. In the winter she is totally happy because we take the old camels inside and leave her outside with a small shed. Her coat grows back and she spends her days, neatly folded up, chewing her cud, at the door of the shed. You would be amazed at the number of telephone calls we get from irate citizens about that camel. They think she's mistreated. They drive by the park on Route 95 and see her alone in the snow and tell us, "That camel should be taken inside." We point out that camels in Afghanistan thrive at much lower temperatures. And I know that they care more about that camel than about the bums and bag women in Kennedy Plaza. I do, myself. Perhaps I like her more than I do Carl. I certainly know her better.

"I remember that coat." Carl touches the sleeve. He was always entertained by texture. You could keep him quiet by giving him cloth scraps. He lost himself in plaids and quilts, studying the designs, touching and stroking. It drove Mom crazy, of course. "And that handbag. Plastic, trying to look like pigskin. I gave her a good leather purse once, and I found it put away in its box marked Best Handbag. Too Good To Use. So what's inside? What treasures?"

"Just the canceled bankbooks. We're supposed to look at them. Nothing in any of them now, of course. She timed it well. Lasted to use up every penny. And then went on state assistance. She never knew that, or pretended not to."

The bankbooks are fragile, like toys in our hands. All different shapes and faded colors. Inside are columns of figures, boldly scratched in broad-nibbed pens: deposit $12.50, balance $91.61, interest $9.16, withdrawn $99.77, account closed. You don't make much in the paper business out of quarters and dimes. That's what happened to Nickel Nelligan's Notions.

I remember, "Once when I was home and you were about seven and learning new words, we were sitting here after supper, and you asked me, 'Are we millionaires?' It was one of the few times she ever laughed. Right out loud. She used to put her hand over her mouth because her teeth were bad. And then you asked, 'Well, if we're not millionaires, are we paupers?' And she must have told you to stop being silly."

"She was always telling me, Money talks. But I could never find out what it was saying. Nothing I wanted to hear." He stubs out his cigarette. "Oh, it's all gone to moth and rust, as they say. Too much past is worse than none."

"She did her best with us. She tried hard."

"And that was the problem. She shouldn't have tried so hard. It wasn't worth it."

"I think I'll keep this coat. I may grow into it. Why don't you see if there's anything in his closet for you."

"Remember she used to say, worst investment you could have, a closet full of clothes." But he runs up the stairs.

My teeth are chattering, not so much from cold as plain dread. The zoo and my warm apartment seem as distant as pinpricks in a night sky. I have to hurry back before they disappear.

In a few minutes Carl shouts, "Come here. Look at me. The last of the Nelligans." He is in the hallway, trying to see himself in the little dark mirror. He has put on Dad's one good suit. The coat sleeves hang over his fingertips. He has hiked up the pants and tucked them over the belt. He looks like a child in a historical pageant. He sniffs the lapels. "His smell. Kind of a mix of sweat and bay rum and Camels." He lifts a matchbook out of the pocket. "The Shell Chateau. My, my! When did he ever get to go there? They never ate out, did they?"

"They might have liked to but didn't dare."

"What stopped them?"

"Themselves. Their own rules. We don't visit. Don't eat out. Don't buy new clothes. Don't stay overnight anywhere. Don't make wills. Almost don't die."

"Here's something you don't know. They got swept off their guard by TV. Right into the mainstream. Each of them had a little black-and-white set, volume turned down low, as if that made it more virtuous."

"By the time she got to the Manor, she stopped watching. Refused to get involved in anything—the bingo or the crafts. Sat waiting, ramrod stiff in her good chair, her respectability intact. Waiting . . ."

"Not for us."

"Certainly not. For Mr. Death. Say, why don't you take that suit?"

"Not really my style, is it?"

"I meant for Roy. Wouldn't it fit him?" I remember their photo.

"Not his style either. Still, he might fix it up. Thanks." He threw me a quick, sure smile, like a boy's. He twirled in the mirror. "I can't wait to see his face. My legacy."

The Guests

They were better friends a year after the divorce than at any time they had been married. They gossiped on the phone about the stupidity of new and old friends, guessed at the chances of failure of existing marriages, and continued to play all their old games. When they met at big parties, they retreated to the kitchen to compare the people they had brought. On Friday nights they often bumped into each other at the Laundromat, and after folding the familiar sheets, unwilling to end their conversation, they went off to the same Mexican restaurant where they had always sat, heads together, finishing and beginning various stories. A few times they passed up the Mexican place for the Pancake House in the shopping mall; from a bay-window table they could stare at the strolling families and laugh at the clothes and hair and walking styles, and sometimes supply dialogue. They were good mimics: Dave had a good ear for subtle dialect, and Sue did neat refinements.

Years ago her high-school drama coach had moaned after Sue had skipped three pages of her only scene in the class play, "You're a far better actress off stage than on." She had never agreed with that description. "I simply can not believe that this is happening to me," she was fond of saying. "How did I ever get into this? It's not what I meant at all."

Before the divorce she had developed a habit of looking over her shoulder and blinking slightly as she slid out of one scene into another. He had taken to sleeping through most of the weekends. Now they never referred to the classic evening battles, when he had shouted, "What do you want? What in hell would make you happy?" He hadn't expected an answer, but he had continued. "Answer me. What am I to you? What do you want of me? She had never thought to ask him what he wanted. She had exhausted all the possible tricks.

"Don't hide from me," he thundered unnecessarily.

"How can I?" she asked, trapped a few inches from his fierce eyes. The neatly patterned black hairs of his arms against the pillowcase seemed to reproach her.

Anyway, that was all behind them now. He got the waterbed, the Norfolk pine, and exactly half the record collection. She took the Castro, the schefflera, and the Cuisinart. They kept their friends. During the process of dividing what they owned, they became interested in each other again.

It was during the next winter that they began meeting, first one day in a cheese store, which led to her inviting him for fondue with three other couples at her place. After the others had left, they spent one of the best evenings they had ever had, discussing his parents, who, it turned out, had not been told about the divorce at all.

He said, "I'd meant to bring it up on the phone, but it never seemed to be the right time. It isn't that they'll be upset. You know that. Why, they probably thought about divorcing, themselves, years ago. Still, there was always some obstacle when I tried to introduce the topic. I thought it ought to have some kind of build-up, like a frame actually."

"I suppose they're still planning to sell the house and move to San Diego. And they're wondering if they'll be happier dying in California than in Idaho," she said.

"Exactly. They're afraid of waking up one morning and finding themselves on big tricycles, pedaling off to bingo in the clubhouse. They'd love it, of course, but they think that giving up that mansion in Twin Falls for a condo in Chula Vista is some kind of moral failure." Dave looked down at the plastic cow pitcher. They had just finished a Whopper Burger after the Ice Capades in the Civic Center. The edges of the parking lot were scalloped with gritty March snow. "Have you noticed?" he asked her. "It's like the end of the world. Everybody is trying to go everywhere before we get grounded for keeps when the light and heat run out and we put cars up on blocks. You know what I'd like to do?"

"No," she said in some remote voice out of another role.

"Drive across the country for one last time. Out one way, back another. See the folks on the way. Get that over."

"That way you'd have something to tell people when they ask about the summer. Seems like a lot of work to give a short answer."

"The only problem is, I really don't want to go alone. Why don't you come?"

"Wouldn't that seem a little funny?"

"Oh, who cares. We always got on better when we were traveling. Remember? Think of yourself climbing Pike's Peak or feeding the bears at Yellowstone or getting up at four a.m. to see the sunrise over the Mojave."

The first year they had been married they had driven west on the TransCanada Highway, most of the time at seventy-five miles an hour, for great stretches seeing only sky and wheat. There were no guard rails. Between them and the wheat was a soft gravel bed. Occasionally above them the rolling white clouds darkened, lowered, and drenched the land, then suddenly lifted, sucking away the moisture. One motel was carpeted entirely in Dress Stuart tartan. They ate Chinese smorgasbord. They visited a pioneer museum and walked inside the sod house, studied a collection of spittoons, stared at group photos taken in 1890 of formally dressed families standing in muddy fields with their dogs and cows at the sides.

On the road their only responsibilities were to keep their sunglasses polished, to check the oil and tires, and to feed themselves and the car. They were happiest in motion, twelve hours straight across Route 40 from Fort Smith through Oklahoma City into Amarillo and on to Albuquerque, the saliva drying, the eyes gritty even under sunglasses. Truck-stop food: a short stack, cheeseburgers, bear claws, broasted chicken, wild blueberry pie, grain-fed steer beef, chuck-wagon hot, all you could eat. Sassy waitresses with name tags and rosettes of handkerchiefs: "Hot up your coffee? Sunny side up? Katsup? Pie with?" The check smartly snapped down on the counter; "Goodbye, Beth, Lula Mae, Doreen, Hazel, Topaz." Across the oil-streaked parking lots past the giant rigs back into driving position, pointing west through Gallup, Winslow, Flagstaff, headed toward Needles or Yuma. They hated to pull in for the night. What was beyond the next bend, over the incline, fifty more miles along? They had covered these routes so many times they were merged in one unnumbered interstate.

So she agreed, and the first day of their summer vacation they buckled themselves into his VW and began boring across the Massachusetts Pike and up the New York Thruway to Buffalo and onto the Ohio Turnpike. It was a weekend, and the traffic bunched only near the bigger cities. They neither ate nor tried to get gas at the plazas, which seemed ravaged, but turned off where they could find diners and watch the truckers.

After breakfast in Fredonia they had their first major fight. After that, they drove on silently for a while and then began to pick up hitchhikers as buffers between them. The first one was a very old man with his collie and three patched shopping bags. When it was her turn to drive, Sue watched the old man through the rear mirror, protected by her dark glasses. He was sucking on an orange, afraid to move his jaws. His dog panted softly out of a bit of window. They were used to silence, as if they would fill less space and make fewer memories by not moving.

The old man got off at the last Cleveland exit; at the end he grew talkative. He had worked ships on Lake Erie for fifty years and was going to try living with a daughter in Lorain. "It probably won't work out. I've run through my whole family," he said. He gave them each a card listing fifteen verses in the New Testament in which oranges had been eaten. "They say fruit in the Bible, but I know they meant oranges. They just didn't want to insult bananas and watermelon." After he left, the car smelled of oranges for a while, and he was something to talk about.

Until Omaha the other passengers were short trippers. Usually at the last exits of cities—Toledo, South Bend, Joliet, Davenport—a dozen or so would be scattered, inviting a choice. Sue and David never had to be alone. As soon as passengers left, others appeared. They never picked up more than two at a time, avoided those with large suitcases, preferred young to middle-aged men and women to men. Actually, there were few women traveling alone, but at Elkhart a solid, ageless woman paused, hand on the door, studying their faces. "I wanted to see what you were before I got in. I do this all the time and I gotta be careful. See, I'm married and I don't believe in adultery. I could run into trouble. There's a lot of peculiar people around." David and Sue stared at her. "You're all right, I guess," she said and got in.

As new guests settled in, new voices and smells insinuated forward. The sleepy silent ones with backpacks created their own isolation, walling themselves in, offering thanks when they got in and left, staring out their windows or nodding off. Dave and Sue talked past and around the strangers and did not quarrel. When the guests in the back seat slept, they whispered like conspirators in the front seat.

After Grand Island, Route 80 stretched grandly over the rolling landscape. Tightly planted soybean rows and quivering corn carpeted the ground as far as they could see. Occasionally, robot irrigators tended their fields. At ten- or twenty-mile intervals skinny roads took off at right angles to invisible small towns: Cairo, Ravenna, Heartwell, Merna. A few years ago on the same stretch they had spent the night in such a town with one hardware store, one donut shop, one main street, and one tiny public library. They had used that town a great deal on conversation the next year. In the donut shop, they had listened to the alfalfa growers describe various slow deaths they knew about—asphyxiation in a silo, mutilation by a combine, drowning in a deep artesian well, goring by a bull.

This time they were being entertained by a young Canadian bound for L.A. who played his harmonica from Lexington to Ogallala. He laughed easily and bought them cones of bubble gum ice cream when they stopped. They giggled a lot. The heat was magnifying their silliness. They dropped the Canadian off, on his way through Utah toward the Pacific.

As they drove toward Cheyenne, the hot day exploded into tired thunder storm. The wipers flashed across the misty windshield, and from the radio, in bursts of static, Loretta Lynn suffered through her losses. For a stretch of flat highway past Sidney they seemed alone, the opposite highway lanes hidden at some distance. Far ahead of them was an unsubstantial overpass like a mirage. Closer, they saw a dark mound of people and objects clumped under the supports.

"Let's not pick them up," she said. "Too much stuff to carry."

"Nobody else will. There's no traffic," he said.

So he slowed and stopped neatly beside the shapes in the temporary darkness. There were two people standing close together, a foot locker, and a tightly packed giant duffle bag.

"You were right," Dave said, too late. "They won't be able to load all that into the back seat."

But they did. The taller figure tossed his arms free of his poncho and shoved the locker and bag into most of the back seat with a small space into which he squeezed himself.

"There isn't much room for your son," Dave said.

"She's my wife," the man said. "She can fit in."

The girl perched sideways between his arm and the car window and spoke up. "I'm Dawn. Really Crystal Dawn, but I go by Dawn. And he's Rod, short for Roderick. All his brothers have names beginning with *R*—Raymond, Robert, Ralph, Roland."

"Shut up!" Rod said.

The girl's lips tightened and she stared straight ahead.

"Were you waiting long?" Sue asked.

Rod nodded and shut his eyes but not completely, as cats and dogs sleep.

Giant double rigs and PIE trucks slapped and splashed the VW. Until Laramie the road surface was littered with scraps and rinds of enormous tires, plastic sheets, fragments of mufflers, discarded sneakers.

When Rod began to snore heavily, Sue looked into the back seat. Dawn leaned forward. "He's dead tired. Hasn't slept since Toledo. We was riding in one of them big rigs."

"How come you got left out back there in the middle of nowhere?" Dave asked.   ·

"Oh, there was some kind of scrap. Rod gets mad if anybody starts being fresh with me." She shrugged. "You got work?"

They both nodded.

"Well we don't. That's why we're trying to find something. Traveling around, trying to find something."

"What can you do?"

"He wants me to stay home, but I'll take anything for money: waitressing, baby-sitting, short order. He worked the pipe line, and before, all kinds of places, like carnivals and circuses a lot. He's got scars from lions, even." She raised the poncho cautiously. Amid the dark hair of his forearms were long and wide white lines which interrupted two tattoos, a dragon and a rose with a name. Dawn pointed to the rose. "That's not my name on it. Some other girl he knew before. He's got another one with my name on it somewheres else. It's a heart. You got a house?"

"No, we live in the city," Sue answered.

"When we get work, we're going to get a trailer, a double wide. We're going to get a dog and a yard and then I guess we're going to start a baby. Right in this locker is a whole set of real dishes. I'd show you, except he'd wake up."

On the radio Dolly Parton lamented her good men gone too soon. Dawn's small voice insisted. "I'm going to have a mailbox with our name on it out front. I bought the fancy letters for it already. They shine in the dark. Did you see Elvis laid out? I mean in the paper. He looked beautiful, not fat at all. I got that picture framed right in that sack. Whenever we get to sleep proper in a bed, I take it out and put it on the bureau to look at. Awful things in the papers. I don't read them none, except the pictures. You want to see pictures of us when we was married?"

Sue looked back without answering. Dawn drew out a turquoise wallet and opened the photo section. "I had four bridesmaids. See, all pastel colors. I got that hat come down over my face. You noticed I got this skin condition on my forehead so I had to hide it. Well, anyhow, that was when we got married."

Past Laramie, for the next 150 miles all the signs announced Little America; wooden penguins told about its eighty gas pumps, rooms, restaurants, shops, all open twenty-four hours. Every five miles or so another sign offered something different: moon rock jewelry, Idaho sheep skins, square beefalo burgers, Indian baskets, mystery grab bags.

"How about checking it out?" Dave asked.

"Let's," Sue said. "We should eat something."

"What about them?" Dave glanced back. Dawn and Rod had fallen asleep, their clothes blended. In their lap was a greasy paper bag. Dave said, "We could invite them to eat with us when we stop. They probably haven't had a hot meal since they left."

"Can you imagine traveling around like that?" Sue said. "Carrying everything you own in a locker and never getting to wash."

"They've got Elvis framed. What else do they need?" Dave said.

The parking lot at Little America shone with dozens of Air Streams on tour, hundreds of rust-and-rain-speckled cars from every state, dozens of trailer rigs that had passed them long ago, and motorcyclists clawing through their saddle bags.

Dawn and Rod had awakened and were whispering to each other.

Dave said, "We're stopping here a while. We'd like you to have dinner with us. I mean, we'll pay."

Rod said, "We'll get out. Look the place over."

"I'll bet there's a lot of pretty things inside," Dawn said. As they walked toward the restaurant, she ran her fingers over as much of the merchandise in the gift shop as she could touch: candles, artificial flowers, fake feathers, incense boxes, glass beads.

Rod studied the menu carefully, moving his thumb down the right column studying the prices. "I'll have a steak, medium rare," he told the waitress, "and she'll have the same." He pointed to Dawn.

Later he winked, jerking his head toward the waitress and speaking to Dave, "I sure would like to see her in a topless bar."

"Hey, quit talking like that," Dawn giggled. "He's always trying to rile me up."

Rod bent over his plate and ate with a minimum of chewing. "Wrap that up," he told Dawn when he saw that she had not finished her steak. He ate the rest of her French fries. He ordered another beer.

"Gee, I'd love some of those licorice candles and one of those cute frogs with sequins for eyes," Dawn said. Rod buttered the last rolls, covered them with napkins, and put them in a bag with the steak. He got up. "I'll be in the car," he said. Dawn followed him.

"And now what do we do with them?" Sue asked Dave. "How do we get rid of them? We can't drop them off here, can we?"

"They certainly are bad news," Dave said.

When they got back into the parking lot, it was dark. Flashing neon signs and the lights of departing cars cut little rays into the intense Wyoming night.

"Look, we'll take you as far as Echo," Dave told them. "Then we have to go north to Idaho."

There was no response from the back. They drove silently on for several minutes. The smell of licorice drifted forward. Sue turned. "Oh, you did buy a candle."

"We helped ourselves to some," Dawn said. "Everything costs so much, taking things is the only way to get even."

"Shut up," Rod said, slapping her hard on the mouth.

"You didn't have to hit her," Dave said.

"Mind your own business. We don't need you to tell us what to do."

Dave slowed down and stopped the car. They seemed to be the last people left in Wyoming. An aromatic grass smell came from the violet silence.

"You drive us to the next exit," Rod said, leaning forward, clenching Dave's shoulder. "I'm warning you. Leave us proper. Start up the car."

Dave drove very fast to the next exit, while Sue stared at the headlights eating up the distance. At the next intersection they stopped again. Sue sprang out to push the seat forward and let them out. Rod pushed past her, dropping the footlocker and duffle on the pavement. He was sweating heavily. He pulled Dawn out of the back seat by her arm. Sue got back inside.

Dawn poked her small face back into the car. "I hate you. You didn't even treat us like human beings. I heard you talking about us when you thought we was sleeping. Just like we was animals. What do you think you are? Why, I bet you aren't even married."

She raised her hand and threw something back into the car. Dave gunned the engine, and they swerved away. Sue looked back as the figures disappeared. She could no longer see their clenched fists or sneers. The smell of licorice candle was overpowering. She reached back and threw it far out into the aromatic grass as they drove swiftly on.

A Thin Place

Weather in this country moves west to east; people, east to west. In the center they meet and nod, but by the time they reach the oceans on either side, they're all used up. When they've moved that far, they've run out of country.

Long ago Fran lived in a green place. In her dreams she walks under tall, healthy elms beside white picket fences. Even in Ohio she never lived in such perfection. Then was Nebraska, then Denver, and now, finally, the Great Basin.

She owns a double-wide metal box tied down to a sloping half acre of desert soil. She has read that twenty-five thousand live in this place, Orchard Valley. She knows the names of three of them. The valley looks too small for twenty-five thousand people. It is actually illegal to build a house here. This suburb is exclusively for trailers and their support systems. The wind blows too much for trees, except low growths that bend away from the mountains. Wild poppies and roses and some fierce grasses do well.

The valley is a violent place, although a silent one. It is like Mars and the moon. Trailers catch fire and, like torches, plume toward the blue sky. There is only a concrete slab left by the time the fire engine arrives. At night county sheriffs' cars, lights strobing, shoot along the feeder roads, stop in a splay of gravel. Then, after an interval, someone in handcuffs crosses the headlights and bobs stiffly into the squad car. In the daytime toy ambulances far down on the main road leading into the valley play out a rescue scene. All these episodes occur silently. Fran sits on her porch, which runs the length of the trailer, staring at the whole valley. Under this enormous sky she has never learned to gauge distance—a thousand feet, five miles.

Few people sit outside or stare into the valley, although everyone has a grand view. They are at work amusing themselves. They collect rocks, cut, polish, and then store them in coffee cans. They make mosaic tables of broken glass. They paint decoy ducks. They learn new steps for disco dancing. They change their cars often, dealing up or down. They are busy.

To keep track of all the rock clubs, dancing lessons, craft shows, and yard sales there is a giant community bulletin board in the shopping center. A thick tabloid printed on orange paper, *The Li 'l Rocket,* advertises darkroom equipment, tap-dancing shoes, Scientology courses, oak tables, rifles, exercise machines, sets of drums, barely used with original boxes and warranties. The *Rocket* has a mammoth circulation. Stacks of them melt from the supermarket entrance on Fridays. On the counter of the café Fran finds dismantled pages with certain items torn out or circled. She reads every item even though the print is very small and smudges.

Occasionally on a Sunday, when she has not heard a voice all day, Fran checks out several of the ads for living-room sets or tooled saddles. It takes surprisingly long to drive to other sections of the spread-out, flat city. Usually the encounters are inconclusive—a life she doesn't want to enter, people she doesn't need to know who are worse off than she. They may not have wanted to sell the objects any more than she wants to buy them. These trips give her purpose as she sets out. She is always glad to come back to her porch, having escaped. But somewhere in the valley there must be someone she should meet. Perhaps even now they are moving out. Into and out of the valley every morning on flat trucks come dismantled halves of trailers. Is she missing someone? Is someone valuable arriving? There should be some clearing house. How would that body have felt or smelled that is now being carried away forever?

Beyond the *Li 'l Rocket* there is not much reading in the Valley. She has been living there four years. She brought books from Denver, Nebraska, before that, even Ohio—long, nicely printed novels and thoughtful essays written from settled lives in well-defined places where history softly wrapped the houses. Sometimes she lies in her hammock and tries to get through a chapter, but something always distracts. She is on the direct flight lane for the planes coming into the city. They float by, their wheels descending for landing, their insignia clear. They too are surprisingly quiet. She watches them, losing her place in the book. The shifting light on the opposite range holds her, frightened and wistful. A few cedar trees on one ridge remind her of a slice of a Florentine landscape seen through a desert saint's window. But no painting or photograph can get this color and light. Her eyes are always taking pictures. When they return to the page, the print squirms and blurs.

It occurs to her that perhaps only Indians should live here, but those that drift in from the reservation own shacks on the dusty southern part of the city, their failed cars and large dogs guarding whatever is inside the closed Venetian blinds. Near them, Mexicans are noisier and cook summer meals out of doors under the chinaberry trees near the coulee. Fran would like to walk near their fires to look into the women's flat faces and hear their rapid talk, but the dogs charge her as she tries to sneak past. Anyone on foot upsets the families, and they stare nervously at her. Even strange cars driving slowly through these terraced hills are eyed by dogs and bands of children on their bikes. Her car is known and accepted on her road. Two roads over, she is an intruder.

"Oh, I'm not complicated," Fran announces, quite correctly. She opens her mouth widely when she talks, and it is a clean red mouth with good teeth. Her skin is still the same everywhere, unveined, softly fuzzy. Depending upon their age, men call her Kid, Pal, Sweetie, Honey, Fran Dear, but now they begin to say Lady or Ma'am or even You, which would be all right if there were compensations. She once thought that she would come to something; people would read about her interesting life. No one she has ever known personally has become famous. That seems to defy the national average.

Her only real distinction is knowing the places where her life went wrong, although being unable to benefit from the knowledge because the circumstances are never the same again. First was her divorce in Nebraska. It is almost a democratic right to have one divorce. Her marriage had been an extension of childhood and school.

It was true that they had known each other since they were ten years old and in fourth grade. Jack had sat at the next desk and had explained fractions to her. He was a small, neat boy with perfect handwriting, and he seemed never to erase or say he was wrong. She remembers Jack by his neat handwriting. That is all that was left of him. He sends her a card every year on her birthday—woodcuts of flowers or birds, without message, only his name, no return address. She tries to reconstruct his voice.

"We won't be hasty," Jack said. "There's no one else. We only need to go our own ways and see what will happen."

Wanting to show resolve, she said, "I will get the divorce then." It gave her a sense of purpose to run around and settle matters as if she could figure out what had gone wrong. What had gone wrong, Jack told her, was that he had grown in a different direction.

"Tell me where you've grown. I'll get there too," she had said, unashamed. Or perhaps she hadn't asked that outright but only remembered later saying what she thought.

"Don't think so much. You're unnecessarily hard on yourself," Jack said. He had been a psychology major too, although now he taught community planning. "We've known each other too long."

That did not seem sufficient reason to divorce, but she knew better than to protest. "I suppose all this will work out. I may move to Denver."

They were living on E Street, at the corner of Third Avenue, in the small college town in Nebraska where Jack taught. This civilized last talk occurred during a summer rainstorm. Their bungalow was fresh with the smell of crushed petunias and well-mowed lawn. They were holding hands and lying on the Persian rug. How could they be holding hands if they were never going to see each other again?

Of course, the last scene did not happen in the space of one summer rainstorm, but there were no tears or shouts. Calm overtook them. At the end she and Jack were as elegantly polite as old Japanese.

"Don't you want to take the dining room table, the silver, your grandmother's sewing basket, the brass chafing dish?" he asked.

"No, none of it," she said, which was a lie. And then, "I'll take the terrarium and the dog. And the Persian rug." Perversely, these were the most difficult objects to carry. The terrarium dried out in Denver; perhaps it couldn't stand the altitude. Perhaps it knew when to give up. The Labrador, called Sable, had loved the big green field in Nebraska.

He had a rough time adapting to Denver and took to walking close to buildings and shuddering. Finally he became resigned.

After a while in Denver she met Carl at the reference desk of the library where she worked. She won and lost him by too much eagerness. He asked for one book on spiders. Through interlibrary loan she found twenty and served them up in a great stack.

"My God, woman, I only wanted to copy one good picture of a spider for a birthday card. I sent the card off a week ago anyway."

She sighed. He never told her whose birthday card. But for all that effort he had to take her home for coffee. He was renting the whole second floor of a big Victorian house with little furniture but lovely parquet floors that framed the Shah Abbas rug when he let her move in. The settled life seemed to cheer Sable. It was the best time of her life. That was in the early 1970s before she got spooky. Even though the nation was suffering, she floated in honey peace as if drugged.

She was able to lose herself, not only with Carl, but with all the sweet drifters passing westward through the city, clomping up the stairs, settling in for the night, grateful for a night's shelter. They were all somewhat younger than she, about Carl's age, but in the marches and protests and shared intensity no one was counting age. Where had all of them gone with their gentle urgency which she could not trust again? At first they sent cards with cryptic explanations: Marge and I split. The kids are with her. Things haven't worked out very well for me. Bucky died in a cycle accident. Imagine me selling insurance!

Carl was tiring of her, but she would not let go. She thought of writing him a letter apologizing for her deficiencies, but he might not have discovered a few of them. Also, they were never apart, so a letter would have been pretentious. She suggested that they make lists of what characteristics they found unpleasant and put them in envelopes and exchange them. She knew that he would have listed her staring at him when he ate and not putting the cap back on the toothpaste and being unable to park between the yellow lines. She tried hard to think of something about him she found annoying but failed.

The spooky phase began when she had a miscarriage in the supermarket between the frozen broccoli and the ice cream. Then strangers' faces looked at hers from the bathroom mirror and the screams in the periodical room came from her own lips. For a while she turned on to

Valium. Carl had said he was a marrier but never proposed. It was she who did, finally testing their happiness, but he told her she was too absorbed in him. There was a whole rest of country, he said, and maybe they (but he meant she) should try it. This time there was less to load into the car.

In Orchard Valley Sable has become nocturnal, sleeping through the torrid days and emerging in the windy twilight to sit on the edge of the porch and to pretend in the darkness that he is somewhere else. His eyesight is bad, he has no friends and has cooled toward her. The Shah Abbas rug is probably the only oriental on any trailer floor in the Valley. Fran has stared at it long enough to know every rose and iris and lotus in its garden.

Before Orchard Valley Fran earned her living with her head. Now it is with her legs. After the divorce she dropped out of the psychology graduate program. If her own life was out of control, how could she advise others? For a while she was a bank teller, then a librarian. As a girl she was good at sports, and her body continues to be more dependable than her mind. From the back and in profile, she looks years younger than she is.

"Exactly what is it you do, Fran?" her mother asked on the phone. "You keep the funniest hours."

"What kind of business is it, really?" her brother wondered.

Her final emancipation was in admitting exactly what it was. She went a little out of her way to confess, "I work in a salon, an exercise salon for women. I'm like a gym teacher." Then she waited for what she guessed would be disapproval and was baffled at mild curiosity, even admiration. "You're out on the floor all day? How tired you must get."

Her clients are pretty, faded women with similar first names—Betty, Sandy, Dolly, Bobby—who identify themselves still by husbands or ex-husbands, not by their temporary jobs or where they live. Fran has given up wondering what they are getting their bodies in shape for. They seem a little puzzled or ashamed of being there at all. There are tapes of quiet music accompanying the stretching, wheeling, thudding, padding. The women like best sitting cross-legged at the end of the session, holding their cups of herb tea. Periodically some of the women disappear silently into new marriages or jobs or move away or become discouraged. Fran has plenty of money, a lot of free time, and nothing to think about at the ends of the days. From the brain down, she is in magnificent shape.

The salon is owned by a franchise. To answer the telephone and make out bills, Fran hired a receptionist, Edith, who had moved to this high, dry city to improve her husband's fading health, but it was too late. Now, beached here, she has made a shrine to him in their condo apartment, an alcove of his bowling trophies, in the center of which is an urn with his ashes.

Fran watches her neighbors in the Valley clinically, hoping to learn patience. To the south is a tough-skinned couple with an almost perfect half acre. They have poured concrete everywhere possible and painted it green. The one patch of real grass is decorated with plastic orna- ments: trellises with roses, a family of graduated-sized ducks, a fawn, large toadstools, a white sleigh, and a fountain flowing night and day from a dolphin in a boy's arms. The trickle of water from the dolphin's mouth is eroding their lawn and carrying away the topsoil of all the lawns below theirs. The tough-hided couple might be fraternal twins, from their straw hats to thong sandals. All day they flap about, trim, pluck, wind and unwind garden hose.

To the north lives a secret family of whom only one member is evident—a lumpy boy with inexpressive moon face who rides his bicy- cle several hours a day in dusty ruts around and around his family's double wide. It took Fran almost a year to realize that he was both retarded and deaf. She had seen his lips move but thought he was shouting to a playmate out of view. Although the wind swirled his voice away, she recognized that these were no ordinary words or in a recog- nizable language.

Once when the boy was lost the father appeared at her door. He did not look directly at her. "Have you seen him?" he asked abruptly, gesturing toward the furrows as if the boy were still wheeling through them. Fran shook her head. "He's not strong in the head, but he's harmless. One of us watches him all the time. Wife and I keep different work schedules. He never gives us any trouble. He's our only family."

"It must be hard for you," Fran said. "I don't think he's gone far."

He had only taken off after a runaway horse and was found in a nearby field, standing close to the horse, still holding his bicycle. But after that conversation the man and woman never looked in her direction. They scurried from their car into their back door, avoiding the light, hiding their faces in large shopping bags. Fran has drawn a curtain over the window through which she would have seen the boy circling in the heat of the day.

She has decided that she will never be of deep personal interest to anyone again. It is a summer Saturday morning and she is lying on the porch hammock when, amazingly, Carl telephones. She has not seen him in two years.

"We've got a lot of filling in to do. Things the letters couldn't cover." His voice is easy.

"Where are you?"

"On my way there. About three more hours of driving. Wait up. It'll be worth it."

"Why?"

"I have something important to tell you."

"What?"

"Not on the phone. I have to be there. It's good news."

"Fine. I'll be waiting on my verandah."

Until mid-afternoon she will have to muddle through an ordinary Saturday. Fortunately, she has the laundry to do. Either because they are lonely or do not want to clog their septic systems, the residents of Orchard Valley patronize the Laundromats in the shopping center. Fran always goes to the oldest one, the one without Muzak or TV. There is hardly anything old in the whole city, buildings or people. The few convalescent hospitals and mortuaries are well disguised and the cemeteries are strange, small places. The old and sick are supposed to remove themselves discreetly. Even Fran begins to notice that she is often the oldest person in a store or parking lot.

The cars outside the Laundromat bear distant license plates—Alaska, Florida, Missouri. It is like a caravansary. Fran loads her machine and begins reading *People* and *Newsweek,* which she stockpiles in the car for Saturday laundry visits.

Children swirl up and down the aisles. One stops suddenly in front of Fran, asking her, "Where were you born?"

"I've forgotten. It happened too long ago."

The child scowls, wanting to be taken seriously. "All right," Fran says, "I was born in Ohio."

"That's far. How did you get here?"

"Little by little. The long way." She doesn't add, "failing westward."

The child points to a tall girl with a tense face who is watching two thirty-five-pounders churn through their last cycle. "That's my Dad's old lady, Sherry. She pays me to stay out of the way. A dollar an hour. She's afraid of me."

"Why?"

"I started a fire in the trailer."

"That wasn't very smart," Fran says.

"I know. I hid the fire extinguisher too. That made it harder to put out."

"You're dangerous."

"Only when they mess with me. As soon as I can, I'm going to be a cocktail waitress. I'm eight now." After that declaration, she skids up the aisle, shaking all the machines to see if they may release stray coins.

Fran takes as long as possible to fold her laundry, envying those who can spend another hour extracting, drying, sorting. How to fill the rest of the day without thinking too much? She is too superstitious to anticipate Carl's reason for visiting.

She had bought the trailer for the porch, which an eccentric railroad man had constructed. "I never sit out there. Nothing to look out at, of course," he said. "I had to have something to do so I kept making it bigger. I had all this wood, see, dropped off lumber cars. Well, you can use it for storage, I guess. Put all your old junk out there and a tarp over it and there's all the closet space you women need."

After sudden desert rains, Fran lies in the hammock and smells the cedar beams and the sage. Like the hills and the mineral-rich rocks, the color of the wood blanches and deepens with the shifting light. She has learned to recognize ten tones of brown. In her own head she calls this porch a verandah.

In Ohio the verandah was the broad, unscreened expanse which held a glider and white wooden rockers with royal-blue cushions and white wicker holders for petunias. On Sunday nights in midsummer they often ate supper there on a little old table covered with a blue-plaid tablecloth. The china was only used in the summer. The chairs were of different heights, bottle green with rush seats. It was a great adventure.

"This is a wonderful meal," her father always said.

"It's just cold chicken and biscuits. Same old meal we always have," her mother said. Compliments flustered her.

"We're living like happy peasants, like the farmer in the dell, aren't we? We should always eat out here."

Her mother sighed. "You don't have to carry out all the food and dishes and silver."

"I know. I'm sorry. We should be able to survive out here on the view alone." He waved toward the lake and the more distant emerald hills. "How many shades of green do you see, Franny?"

She was constantly being tested, and she responded quickly, "The maiden hair fern and the petunia leaves on the porch, that grass in front, the nearest ash tree, the next maple, the elm across the road . . ."

"You can say them over silently, dear. To yourself." Her mother usually had migraine.

Long ago, after Fran's mother sold the Ohio house to a dentist for office space, she went off to a condominium in Florida. Their every-other-Sunday telephone calls are monologues for her mother, who has recently had the moles taken off her back. This seems to be in preparation for death, about which she is downright cheery. "They're dropping off like flies down here. I never buy more groceries than I need for the next three days." She has given instructions about burial in a purple pants suit with a flattering blouse in a beautifully landscaped memorial park in Clearwater.

Early in the afternoon Carl drives smartly up in an unfamiliar powder-blue sports car. He hugs her. "Hey, you look great. I like to see you so together. I'm starved for some sleep. You mind? I've got to stretch out for a few hours. Then we talk. O.K.?"

He always fell asleep instantly. Like some extraordinary creature, there he is, sleeping on her Indian spread, the Irish blanket pulled up to his chin. Fran, tiptoeing in to watch him sleep, believes that she has stolen him away like some rare treasure. At the moment before he awakens and smiles at her, she thinks he is the only person who has ever taken the trouble to know her.

"God, I was tired," he says, "It's all that driving through nothing."

"Come outside," she says. "We'll eat cherries on the verandah."

She is pleased that she saved the cherries from a dwarf tree from the birds. They are the first fruit this land has ever yielded, and they have been in the refrigerator waiting for him. She pours them into a grey bowl that Carl made in a pottery workshop in Denver. It has blue cornflowers loosely scattered along their stems.

"Remember this?" She has kept the note he folded into the bowl when he gave it to her in her wallet for years.

"No. Should I?" He does not wait for the answer but places the bowl between his legs as he sits down. "Well, how is it with you out here? Never figured you'd last it out."

"Why not?"

"Whole place is a put-on. Orchard Valley? Hearing that name you'd think of groves sloping down to a river, instead of a big gravel pit."

"There was so an orchard here on the original ranch. The land's too valuable for farming now."

"Too valuable?" he asks, incredulous.

She turns defensive. "People want to live here. It's the second most rapidly growing area in America." She has read this recently.

"What's the first?"

"I don't remember."

"Well, anyway, you seem to have made a life here. I'm glad for you."

She waits, hardly breathing, for him to talk on about their lives.

"I came to give you the good news." He throws a handful of cherry pits over the railing. "I'm getting married, Fran. I'm going to be a husband. To the all-American girl."

"I didn't know they made them any more."

"Stop that. You're not cruel. I don't like your tone. I thought you wanted me to be happy. That's why I broke my ass driving all the way out here. So that you could see how it turned out. You always were a strange one."

I must pull my life together, Fran thinks, realizing that she has made that statement too many times and even doodled it on the telephone directory on several pages under circumstances she can not remember.

"I think we all have to have personal security to get us through," he says. "It doesn't matter what it is as long as it works."

"What do you recommend?" she asks. "Bumper stickers?"

"I don't understand."

"I mean you can learn from bumper stickers: Try Jesus. Have you hugged your kid today? Farmers make better lovers. Your Country, love it or leave it. Or horoscopes: Attend to family matters this Thursday. Give your partner your ear and eye. Fortune cookies: You will receive useful message from old friend."

Carl's stare is chilling. When they lived together, they never talked this way. Now he is streaked with strangeness, the touch and smell of someone else. She knows that she is boring him and doesn't care. Nothing else can go wrong. Once she knew the surfaces of his body better than he did. Now he might flinch from her touch.

"Stop looking tragic, Fran," he says. "You can't try to look like Camille when you're talking about bumper stickers."

"Why not? It's my porch."

"I'm sorry that you're so miserable. You have the capacity for happiness. It's this place that's responsible. It's like living in the departure lounge at Kennedy."

Floating above them is a yellow-and-black-striped plane. The bamboo wind chimes rattle. Carl is so bored that he does not want to argue. His fingers drum the chair arm. She is something to be gotten past. "I have to make a phone call. O.K.? Then I'll be shoving off," he says. "Are you coming inside?"

Fran shakes her head. He always made a ceremony of small actions and he is very graceful to watch. After love, between friendship and nothing, it is wiser to take nothing.

Once she lived in a real house with a large attic, a grape arbor, a root cellar, a cedar closet, a copper beech, a sun dial, and a two-hundred-year-old sampler on the wall of her bedroom. All in a green place.

Now she lives in a thin place with very little between herself and the sky. Orchard Valley is expanding from its basin higher and higher to the tops of its mountains like a bowl filling. New divisions are hinted at by mystery roads that lead up and over the ridges. Where do they end? Fran likes these roads, untouched and waiting.

Someone is always left to go the rest of the way.

A Short Vacation

When the emergency team found Ned Smith crumpled up on his kitchen floor, no one was surprised.

"After the wife goes, they run right downhill," the caseworker announced, gesturing a rollercoaster slide over her clipboard. "Now if it's a woman left, she finds a whole network and perks up. But a man left alone simply shrivels. Like a little leaf." She rubbed her fingers together, crumbling the leaf. "He stops caring for himself and gives up. Especially after sixty years."

"Can you imagine being married sixty years to the same person?" the nurse asked. "Even one year. I wonder what it feels like."

"Boring," said the caseworker.

"Maybe not." The nurse was a romantic but less so every day.

His wife, Emily, had warned Ned Smith not to fall into enemy clutches. He tried to follow her instructions obediently. In the hospital he would not confess to much of anything: his age, his medical history, his financial situation, his religion, his closest kin. He tried to distract the questioners with chatter about the Celtics and motorcycles.

"I'll cut my own toenails, thank you," he told the foot doctor. "I was walking almost seventy years before you were born," he informed the physiotherapist. "You're a nice young man, but you can't do anything for me," he said to the physician. "Why do I have to order from a menu if everything's always the same?" he asked the nurse's aide. "It's time to go home now," he announced on the third day. His gall shocked him. He was quivering inside. What would Em think?

"I don't understand at all," the doctor said.

"What don't you understand?" the caseworker asked.

"What Smith meant when he said he might have a few more months' vacation. He's been retired for years."

"Oh," she said. "He intends to go on living a while. He thinks he's stealing some vacation time away."

"Stealing from whom?"

She pointed upward with her pencil.

"Oh," the doctor said. "From up there. That's one way of looking at it."

On his return trip home, Ned insisted on sitting in the front seat of the ambulance. Before they reached Captain Ed's Chowder House, he bribed the driver to stop for lunch. "My treat."

"We're not supposed to do this. It's against regulations," the driver said.

Ned directed him to park behind the dumpster. They entered through the kitchen. Ned had a dozen oysters on the half shell, two clam cakes, and an order of French fries. The driver had a BLT.

How scandalized Em would be. She knew within a gram the daily potassium and cholesterol ceilings and had the fiber and leafy vegetable requirements worked out. "Now write it down," she would say. "Put on your thinking cap and get this down in your notebook." She had tried to anticipate every problem: a list of what ties to wear with which shirts; how often to change the sheets; whom to call about the furnace; what to give the paper boy at Christmas; the value of money. Odd, he thought. Most widows of his generation had to learn how to handle their checking accounts for the first time. It had been the other way around for them.

Em had gone to business. She was a teller in her own cage at the Thames Savings Bank when he had come to gild the letters over the front entrance. Ned made sure that the job lasted and lasted. She had an enormous respect for money, especially cash. A sort of holy awe glowed around her when she touched new money. "You have no sense of its value," Em said. It was no use reminding her that he had his own square package of fifty sheets of gold, beaten thin as a whisper by wooden mallets. When he was courting her, he had worn his new diamond ring. The old sign painter from whom he had learned the business told him that merchants would respect him if they saw a clear white diamond sparkling on his hand. "Put that away," she had said. "Men don't wear jewelry." He'd have to find that ring and wear it again.

Em selected his clothes. "You have to be careful," she said. "Your taste is undependable." She did not want to hear that he knew fourteen different shades of green and ten of blue.

"Don't tell anyone what you do," she said. "I don't want to be married to a sign painter. Simply tell them you have your own workshop. They may think you're a tool-and-die maker."

Nobody asked the question. Ned might have replied, "Artist. I'm an artist." That wasn't true, of course. He thought it might have been fun to say that he was a half-artist, but he knew better than to say that aloud. He liked driving around the town and seeing his handicraft: Pick Your Own Strawberries. Pies Baked on the Premises. Break It and You've Bought It. That was in the Wee Bit of Scotland Gift Shop. He thought that message was too abrupt, so he added a smiling girl under a tam, shaking her finger.

He had touched up the stuffed tuna and bluefish on the walls of Captain Ed's and the signs for the Gulls and Buoys rooms. He had painted leaping fish over Ed's van.

"I bet they won't give us a bill," he told the ambulance driver.

"Call me Remo," the driver said. "I'm sort of in the arts myself. I'm only driving until we make it."

"How?" Ned asked.

"I'm with a group. Slippery Elm. Ever hear of it?"

"I like the name," Ned said. "But I haven't heard of you. I've led a sheltered life. But I'm going to change that. I'm taking a little time off before I go back to dying."

That seemed to make sense to Remo.

When they got back to the parking lot, Ned supposed it would be too bold to ask if he could drive the ambulance the rest of the way. He did love a good engine. When he shut his eyes, he could remember the sound of every car he'd ever owned and, best of all, the Harley that Em made him sell the day after he bought it. "At your age. What will the neighbors say?" They had already outlasted all the neighbors they knew. They referred to the new ones as the people in the La Frances' and the Robinsons' houses.

They had been married almost twenty years before he tempted her to leave their apartment for a house. She had reservations. Once you put your money into a house, it disappeared into a great swamp. He convinced her that though it was too late for children they could still have a house, their first and last house. They used very little of it, as if the real owners would claim it. But she did clear the yard of trees. "They look untidy. As if we had something to hide." So she ordered him to cut down the Lombardy poplars and the catalpa and then a pear tree and finally the cherry, which attracted birds. He had hoped to train a rose over an arbor in the backyard or, even, Concord grapes. He could make wine. "Wine!" Em scowled. "That's not an American thing to do. You should be ashamed."

Remo seemed in no particular hurry. When they reached Ned's house, he sat in the kitchen and had a can of Moxie. "So what happened to you, anyway," he asked, "that you had to go to the hospital?"

"I was waiting for the mail," Ned said.

"That'll do it every time. The mail is downright dangerous."

"I was just lying on the floor. I would have gotten up eventually. But the woman who delivers the mail—for some reason she wants to be called the mailperson—she saw me and called the emergency unit."

"You think your life's going to be different now?" Remo asked.

"You never can tell. It's not over yet." It seemed to Ned that he had spent such a long time being old that he had not properly grown up at all. He had just gone from being a child in his mother's house to being a child in Em's. It was as if he had skipped over adolescence and middle age entirely. Em had hurried him along. She was always washing the dishes before they got to dessert. She was probably right now sighing over him, drifting from one disaster to another. If he knew where she was, he would have called her up and comforted her.

Finally, after another Moxie, Remo got up to leave. He paused at the screen door. "I'll be seeing you around. If you're ever looking for somewhere to go, we play on Saturday nights at Fred's Steak House on Veasie Street. Decent food too."

The next day the Meals on Wheels began. The meals weren't all that interesting, but the way they arrived was. In blue Rabbits and white Horizons, in Volvos and a Buick LeSabre coupe. "Hello. I'm Bonnie." "Hi. I'm Helen." "I'm Goldie." "What a snug room!" "How tidy you are." "Feeling OK?" They breezed in and out. It was hard to waylay them. He tried. Asked questions about the kids sitting in the parked car, asked about the mileage they got, asked how they kept the food warm, asked how many customers they had. Most of them nervously tried to get out of the house as fast as possible. Maybe they had too many obligations. Maybe they thought if they stayed, they'd catch some of his liver spots or begin losing memory or hair.

One day a silver Dodge Lancer pulled up, driven by a woman in less hurry. She was old enough not to worry about getting older. "I'm Olympia," she said. "I'm sorry. It's chicken today."

"That's all right. It has to be chicken sometimes. Won't you sit down?" he asked.

"Oh, yes, thank you," Olympia said. "What'll it be. Walk or fly?"

"What's that?" Ned asked.

"Oh, I mean will you have a leg or a wing. It was just an expression my husband used."

"I'll fly then. That's a mighty smart car you have."

"Oh, dear, yes. I guess it's a nice car." She looked distracted.

"What's wrong?" he asked.

"This is my first day doing this. I have no sense of direction. Five people are somewhere out there waiting for their chicken, and they may never get it."

"That's no problem," Ned said. "I know this town like the back of my hand. I've painted signs for practically everything here. I can show you where to go." He knew that he was bragging, but he was carried away too far to pull back.

So he sat in the car and gave her directions and handed her the cartons, and they got all the chicken delivered. Their system worked so well, they saw no reason to abandon it. He loved the car, and Olympia was a fine listener.

He told her everything. "Minor characters are appearing in my dreams. Last night I dreamed of Mrs. DeLuca, the seamstress, who knocked over the kerosene lamp and was a pillar of fire before they put a blanket over her. She went back to sewing. Why did I dream of her?"

Ned had seen her kneeling in front of his mother, hemming a new dress. The shiny, clawed hand drew a line of chalk on the navy serge. She took a pin from the row at her lips and attached the hem. His mother turned slightly. He could see his mother's best shoes, well polished but cracked and turned over at the heels. He could not see her face. Even Em's face was fading in his memory.

"Do you think the dead look down or across at us?" he asked Olympia.

"I don't know. I hope they're not unhappy with us."

"Do you know," he said, "I called her My Tame Angel."

"He used to call me, You Old Fossil. He said it gently, though."

"People say things to fill the space a lot of the time."

He remembered that Em had trained him so well that she had only to begin a sentence. She started a lot of aphorisms she never finished. "Give you enough rope . . ." "If you're so smart . . ."

When Olympia and he had delivered all the meals, they went on a drive. Ned leaned back in the contoured plush seat and heard the transmission make its intelligent choices. They were going to the city park to check up on the trees, to see how much further they'd come along. He pointed out the signs he'd made for the bicycle paths. Inside the casino building, he told her, on the carousel were lions and leopards and one unicorn he had touched up every spring, removing the scuffs and nicks left by frantic riders.

"Let's go in some day and watch all the children on the animals," she said.

"You're a good listener," Ned said. "Were you always this way?"

"I guess so," she decided. "My husband was the sure one. He knew a lot of things. The way you do."

"I learned a lot of things. I don't know where all of them are. I used to worry about losing some of them—all those dates and the lists of presidents and battles and parts of the Constitution. Now there seem to be more important things."

They had taken to eating their lunch in the car, parking where there was a good view. Olympia particularly liked the park. "You know," she said, "for the longest time before I met you, my best friends were plants." She spoke too honestly to threaten him.

She put her trust in aloe vera and, she confessed one confidential day, in an adviser in Fall River named Madame Rose. Ned had gently turned down her invitation to visit Madame Rose, but he did try a poultice of aloe vera on his sore knee.

"Let's park here," he told her, under the tulip tree. He had told her that this was his favorite tree in the park. He didn't tell her that he figured it was about his age. Its straight, elephant-colored trunk rose directly up about seventy feet. Its big leaves were pale green gloves. The creamy yellow flower cups attracted masses of bees.

Olympia helped him to cold cuts and potato salad. "I like this tree. There's so much going on," she said.

Life seemed sweeter than he could admit to anyone, even to himself.

"You know," he said, "one of the good parts of being old is that you don't have to sit on the ground in order to have a picnic. You can afford to be comfortable."

Viewing the Remains

It is mid-January and Vivian has made it to the last morning of her visit with her brother, Nick, and his wife, Sue. It is her first visit back here since the transplant.

Vi has only one kidney. Two years ago she gave her other one, the left one, to her brother and so saved his life, or freed him from dialysis. She does not think about the operation; actually she can hardly remember it. He seems to be able to think of hardly anything else. Nick has a perfect memory, especially for scabs and disappointments. Perhaps Vi could remember if she wanted to.

Once, having to catch a train in Spain, she forgot her suitcase on the platform. She jumped onto the moving train and watched the case disappear as the train sped up.

"I would have jumped off and collected it," Nick says.

"Of course, you would have," Vi says. "Old things. You have to get beyond them or they'll strangle you. What did I want with a lot of old clothes?" She does not tell him that she misses all the contents of the suitcase, especially the inlaid pin from Toledo that she never got to wear and the old Clarks shoes, the blue batik scarf, and a clown puppet, the only gift from a man she missed bitterly for years.

She should talk. Bits and pieces of her past are scattered all over Virginia and Michigan and Kansas City and Denver. In attics and closets of friends are lamps and dart boards and blouses and rolled-up canvases and newspaper clippings and books that were supposed to change her life. She imagines fresh starts on islands, in empty houses, even motel rooms, but her discontent surfaces and finds the flaws as a tongue seeks out a broken tooth.

She keeps on disappointing Nick both when she intends and doesn't. She wonders how he will rate this visit. He's probably already taking stock. They were a family that communicated by anecdote. Vi still thinks during bad days, "I can make a story out of this. Just cut out the nasty parts and point up the irony. It'll do. They'll like it."

If they know about the operation, people assume that she and her brother are close. That was never true. She would never have selected such a brother. She feels vaguely guilty that she can not love him. When the physician called her to describe his kidney failure, she sized up the transplant as a way of getting free of the whole family. They should be even by now. But Nick seems to be living on the margin of her life. He waits to make some declaration.

No decisions are ever easy for him, especially the minor ones. He and Sue debate all the alternatives—Scotch broth or a reuben for lunch, salt vs. calories, if Scotch broth, what brand. Will they drive to town through the ravine (icy but pretty) or past the bakery (quicker and they can pick up some sweet bread). They debate the brands of toothpaste and cat food they will buy as if they are stars in a commercial. They are not performing for Vi's benefit. They would, anyway.

He is a constant worrier about the house. He goes downstairs to check the furnace and the water heater every few hours.

"Doesn't he seem more anxious to you?" Sue asks. "He gets so easily upset."

"Often?" Vi asks.

"No, but it frightens me."

"Is it the medication?"

"They say not. It happens without warning. At night especially. I try not to notice, but he calls out. You remember how it was in the hospital when they had to put him in restraints."

"Actually, I don't," Vi admits. She can't understand, but her entire memory of the transplant, "our operation," as Nick calls it, has been erased: the complicated tests, the visits of cheery friends, the extravagant praise for her, which he mentions. She can not recall the week of recuperation although Nick shows her newspaper photographs of them sitting in wheel chairs in what looks like a hotel room. He tells her that they were in a fancy suite in Mass General, professionally decorated with color-coordinated draperies and bed spreads. He can even remember their color and texture, the menus, what book Vi is reading in the photograph. His hospital memories are especially sharp. The transplant seems to be his central definition.

Since the operation he has been convinced of his Selection. He calls it a Miracle. Saved. He capitalizes these words in frequent letters to Vi, which she skims. At some point in the recovery room he had seen a vision and felt the pressure of an angel's arms pulling him along a high wall at great speed. But something else he could not see clearly stood at the gate further along calling out, "Not yet," in a powerful voice. There were other details of curious smells and sounds which were as difficult to translate as the sound of snow or the taste of mushrooms. Sue, who had been one of his nurses, had actually met him about the time of the vision. Vi supposes that this bonds them.

At any rate, they are born again, evangelical Catholics. They reinforce each other in the same way they share stories and meals. They sample food from each other's plates.

Vi has timed her visit to avoid Sunday mass. Their parents had been automatic Catholics, dressing up and going off to ten o'clock mass and leaving all that conveniently in the parking lot. They were nervous about any reference to Faith. For Vi religion often turns dangerous. She thinks she gives off a scent. It draws preachers and healers. Young men in brown suits appear at the doorway to pray with her. Heavy women with thick glasses and well-marked Bibles approach her while she is holding an ice cream cone. Whenever she moves, she loses friends but is followed by letters from the missions.

"We pray for you," Sue tells her cheerily.

There is no proper answer. Not "Thanks," "Save it," "I sure need that." She settles on, "I only want to be left alone."

"Time enough for that."

"It makes me nervous, talking about belief. I'm probably prejudiced against faith and that's the ultimate sin. But so much of what's called religion seems pretty ugly and selfish to me."

"You get past that soon," Sue says.

"That's what I'm afraid of."

"It's like coming home when you've been away on a long trip."

Sue means every word she says. She gives out signals when she is going to shift the topic. She touches the hem of her dress or picks a phantom thread from her cuff. She smells of Clorox.

The night before, she said, "You have such aristocratic names—Nicholas and Vivian. And me stuck with Susan."

Vi does remember suddenly. "You know Nick's confirmation name is Bede."

"Who was he?" Susan wants to know.

"Oh, it was on account of Nick's birthday, May 27th."

"But what was Bede?"

"Some holy man. Venerable. Read a lot."

Susan will put away all those facts like baby teeth or report cards. Vi is thinking of the day of their confirmation in Attawagan. Probably 100 degrees in a packed church, all of them holding white pieces of cardboard with their saint's names in elegant calligraphy. Several children fainted before getting up to the bishop's chair and were carried out to lie on the lawn and fanned a little and then marched back inside.

They are trying hard to make this visit work. Last night Nick brought out the photo album and, encouraged by Vi's show of interest, he decided that they should look at some home movies—their parents' wedding, the reception under a striped tent at the Elks Club, their mother throwing her bouquet into a swarm of wasp-waisted bridesmaids, she waving from the decorated front door on their first Christmas on Samuel Slater Crescent, then all of them cooking breakfast when they camped at Beach Pond, their parents dressed as General Greene and his wife on a float at the Bristol Parade, lifting champagne glasses at some anniversary party, in lobster bibs at a clam bake at Rocky Point.

"It's too bad they're not here right now," Sue says.

Nick and Vi stare at her. If it were not for hair and skin, you could almost stare directly into her head and see all the busy nerve cells making connections. She is best in emergencies and should be saved for them, Vi thinks.

"Do you hear much from Mom and Dad?" Nick asks.

"Not a lot. As much as necessary," Vi answers.

"I don't understand. They don't seem to keep in touch as much as we'd like," Nick says.

"They probably don't take care of themselves down there," Sue says.

Their parents are in better shape than they've ever been. "We deserve our freedom now," their mother says. Smiling to themselves, they drove to San Antonio, bought a prefabricated house, and had it set up that day on a slab in a retirement community. She does needlepoint bell pulls for Christmas. He's qualified as a masters' broadjumper. They have two bedrooms and say that they're sorry that they have no guest room. "You don't have to worry about us. We're on our own now, doing what we want," they say.

"I wonder what it is that they want. What do they do all day, do you think?" Nick asks Vi.

"She is tuned into 'The Young and the Restless' and smoking her head off, and he's snoring away in front of 'M*A*S*H' in his room. Then they'll go off to Taco Bill's. Or maybe she's doing a short course at Gloria Stevens and he's making the third perfect Margarita. They've earned it."

Nick says, "I have this odd feeling, Sis, that they blamed me for getting sick on them. Like I showed them up as genetically defective. Do you remember how spooked they were by the hospital? It seemed that they stayed away from both of us until we were recovered or almost."

"But what could they do for us?" She does remember them larking into the room in matching green-and-white outfits, wanting to be admired. Their shoes were very white; they were well tanned and trim. They sucked in their stomachs and walked smartly like tap dancers. Their arms are full of magazines. They were on parade and didn't want to hear about hemostats and jaundice or renal failure and rejection. They deserved two kids with perfect bodies and describable occupations.

Instead, they have Vi teaching in a collapsing private school nobody ever heard of and Nick making a career out of recovery. He dropped out of college, then back in, finally out of law school, avoiding failure like a cat mincing over a brook on flat stones. He's bought into one franchise after another. The last was water beds. His garage is full of fancy headboards and packets of antibacteria fluid and sky-blue booklets describing the wave action. Right now, he is getting ready to be a health-food distributor.

"We're very busy," Nick tells Vi. "Sue works and I save." He has not bought anything at full sticker price for years. He shows Vi his coupons under general headings: Cans, Soups, Soft Drinks, Soap. He describes mill outlets and yard sales.

Sue is a sport about conversation. She believes in fair play. "And how do you live, Vi?" she asks.

"What do you mean? What is it you want to know?"

"Tell us about your school."

"Well, it's like most such places."

"You've been there some time. You used to move around more," Sue says.

Vi tries to fix on some satisfying detail. "It's in a meadow." Originally, it was a big old wooden resort hotel in a canyon on a river. The whole place is falling apart. Even with the Kuwaitis and foreign service kids and the head-hunting service, enrollment drops every term. Each payroll is more dubious. The faculty take turns cooking for the students on weekends. The Saturday work details are dead serious projects like plumbing repair and shingling. Unless they put in a sprinkler system and hire a real science teacher and fix the cracked tennis court and borrow twenty thousand, their accreditation will run out next month. Vi suspects that the students know the school is on the skids and may close before graduation.

"I may be somewhere else next year," she says.

"They wouldn't fire you, would they?" Nick looks alarmed.

"No. Enrollment problems."

"Not enough warm bodies at the fancy prices?"

"There's some uncertainty. It's not all that expensive."

"You have good students?"

"All kinds. A mix. They get a decent value."

What sticks in her head right now is the face of a Nigerian who tried to burn the place down when he heard he'd be deported. Eighty percent of his body is covered with second-degree burns. No one can figure out who is responsible for his medical bills. The best student is the fifteen-year-old daughter of an oil company executive whose home address has changed ten times in the last year. On any form asking nationality, she leaves a blank. She is a compulsive eater and stores food in her room. She has an IQ of 150 and throws up after every meal.

"You teach languages?"

"Yes, a little history and Spanish." Her Spanish is sloppy. She has a good ear but lacks discipline. Might have earned a decent living if she could cut out the booze and grass. Loses people and years and chances. Hasn't had a drink in the last three days. She thinks about herself as little as she can. Recently the brightest student, cornered, shouted at her, "I know all about you. You're a stupid old drunk. An easy lay. If you were any good, you wouldn't be in this cruddy school."

"Do you still live in a dorm?" Sue asks.

"No. I share a place with another teacher, a few miles down the river." She has moved into a trailer with the school's business manager, who also teaches math. His wife, who taught art, split for San Francisco last summer. He never noticed her until she left. Now the trailer is a museum: her old grey sweater, her cigarettes, her dental floss, her pine cones in a sweet-grass basket. It is spooky. He sleeps with Vi, but they do not make love. No one believes this, and she is ashamed, but they are both too lonely and tired to talk about it.

Perhaps because he likes company, he never turns off the radio, although the volume is so low that only high notes or squeaks or muttering comes through. He will not shut drawers and leaves doors ajar. The school's accounting is never finished. By the time she returns, someone else may have moved in. She will miss the dog, a neat, decent collie who only asks to rest his chin on her knees and to stare at her. She will leave behind some shoes or shirts for the museum. The school will shut untidily with no warning. She will collect unemployment for twenty-six weeks and read through Iris Murdoch and lose twenty pounds.

A grandfather icicle crashes from the kitchen window. Nick goes out to inspect. Then he begins taking his medicines. They are in an attaché case, fitted out like a medical picnic basket. Inside the cover is a schedule. Then he disappears to work out in the garage. There in the half light amid the water bed remnants he lifts weights and skips rope. Vi remembers that she used to fall over him sitting in the dark, talking to himself, when he was a boy.

"It's good for him. He needs to release some of the tension," Sue explains.

"You're quite remote out here, aren't you?" Vi says.

"We bought in the summer. Everything seems closer then, you know.

We thought that we'd have a lot to do together out here. When we came out for a last look with the agent, we really got taken in. Hanging geranium baskets, fresh trim, the smell of apple pie baking."

"And then you found out that the nice family had borrowed the flowers and they were burning cinnamon in the oven."

"Oh, no," Sue says. "It wasn't that bad. Anyway, the closets are wonderful, and the lawn's easy maintenance." She stares down at her rings. They are too serious and old fashioned for her to have bought them. "You're looking at this moonstone. It belonged to Mabel Rennick, who ran the New Frontier Bar and Grille in Kennedy Square. I wear it in her memory. She suffered wonderfully, and we had a good time together. Poor lady. She tried hot packs and herbs and faith healers, but finally she put herself entirely in my hands. She had no one at the end. That's what I worry about us."

"You could get a dog," Vi says.

"Oh, no. If things were different, perhaps a child. I could, you know, but Nick shouldn't, and he wouldn't think of adopting."

"Well, a dog's safer," Vi says. "You have a better idea how they'll turn out. And they don't last as long."

"Wouldn't you like a child?"

"No. I feel I've had too many of other people's children."

The conversation freezes. Vi decides it's not worth thawing. She is growing more silent every day. Teaching frightens her. Her heart thumps before classes begin, and she is always relieved to discover that she's lasted out the fifty minutes.

She hears the furnace surge; two minutes later gushes of hot air come through the floor vents. The cat jumps down from his usual chair, stretches his back, and falls against a vent. He is a sad, silent cat named Fur, a gray tiger. Doors are left open so that he can drift like a solid shadow through the house. At night he lumbers over Vi's legs, stretches with a sigh in the center of the bed, but he vanishes dissatisfied in a few minutes. His sounds are limited to occasional sighs and loud crunching of his dried food.

"Before you go," Nick says, "we must take you to Harvestland."

"What's that?" Vi asks.

"The biggest supermarket in three states. It's a kind of food theme park."

"It's an exciting place," Sue says. "Once I saw a husband and wife get into a violent argument in the ravioli. I think one of them was stabbed, but they put up screens around the pasta section until the police came."

"Do we really have to go?" Vi asks. "I'd rather hear you describe it."

"I have to try to complete my game card," Nick says. "I'm looking for another green star to qualify for the Easter drawing." He enters contests, knows all about decorating envelopes and winning techniques for sweepstakes.

"What's the prize?"

"Five years of time sharing in a Miami condo," Nick says.

"He wins lots of things," Sue says proudly. "Out of the garage we have three radios and a case of dog food and a jungle gym and a river raft. We barter away what we don't need."

There is no way of getting out of the last sightseeing tour. The plows have scraped the road and the sun is thinly trying to be cheerful, as is Nick, who suggests, "Let's drive by Samuel Slater on the way." The old house, the one they grew up in on Slater Crescent, was the first ranch house built in town after World War II. The house looks abandoned. There is a tire swing on a ragged rope on the maple in the side yard. A Venetian blind over the picture window has broken and sags crookedly. The mail box is bashed in, and a snow shovel with a torn-off handle is stuck in a drift in front of the garage. "They've had hard luck," Nick says unnecessarily. "Anyway, we had the best of the place. It certainly brings it all back, doesn't it, Sis?"

Vi will never be easy with the past. She is thinking now of the five or six times he emptied her bank and spent the money for candy and of his annoying habit of licking his lips and pulling one ear lobe, still with him. It is absurd, this whole business of talking about blood ties. If she had the guts, she would ask Nick, "What do you want of me? To like you? To select you as a friend? We've been relatives too long. Haven't I earned the right to board up my heart and hang out a sign: Closed. No applications taken."

"You don't mind if we drive past the cemetery, do you?" Nick asks.

Vi wants to shout, "Yes, I do mind. You go, but don't tell me about it." She supposes it is the grandparents that he thinks she should not miss. She paid her debt there too, running errands and listening to the same story thirty times over the same Sunday dinner and making trips to the nursing home where their grandmother, unspeaking, lay clutching a stuffed animal.

They swing out of the Crescent and along Rochambeau Boulevard, past Eisenhower High. The clock over the main entrance has stopped, as it always does in cold weather. The windows of one section of the building are boarded up and covered with spray-painted initials.

Further up the Boulevard amid triple deckers is a pink cement cube about ten stories tall in a snowy field. Nick explains, "That's the high rise—Roger Williams Villa. Housing for the aged. Packed. Waiting list two years long. Full of people you know." She doubts that.

"We visit there often," Sue says. She is sitting between them like a good child, trying not to take up too much of the space. "We have a prayer and healing group that meets in the recreation room. Wouldn't you like to go in?"

"No, really, with bad weather coming I'll just take the supermarket. I don't want to miss my plane," Vi says. She can imagine the recreation room: plastic chairs, cheery signs, tables for bingo, emergency call buttons, some yellow-leafed geraniums, a faint smell of aging.

Past the Elks Club and the Fish and Game shooting range and the frozen reservoir is Gate of Heaven cemetery. There has been no recent burial; the road ways are not plowed. "If we'd worn boots, we could have gone in. That's a pity." Nick stops the car parallel with the family plot. "At least we can look over. It's four stones left of that blue spruce. I come out here quite often." Wind rattles the limbs of the young maples in a row at the entrance and the plastic bows on the old Christmas wreaths.

Sue says, "It does seem lonelier out here in the winter."

They drive on, carefully, over the slick roads to Harvestland. Encouraged by forecasts of an approaching blizzard, hundreds of cars clog its slippery approaches. Police with orange slickers and batons wave new arrivals into distant lots. There is actually a waiting line for admission. The shopping carts are bigger than any Vi has ever seen. Like pygmies, they try to gain respectability by filling the baskets quickly. But Nick is searching for items that will qualify for a green star. Getting a star depends upon selecting at least one item from each of seven categories. An automatic scanning device reads the carts. Vi wishes that she could buy him a green star and be done with it.

She has never felt so small in her life. It is not only the gigantic carts but the double-wide aisles and the towering shelves. At the lowest level are cans in chutes waiting for release. Here and there are curved little stairs to help you reach for the top, where the no-name brands are. A young man in chef's costume and roller skates passes a tray of cheese and crackers.

Nick does not complete the points for the green star. "We'll be back next week," Sue says. "Something new every time. It has a nice atmosphere. I even like to read the notices on the bulletin board. You find out what's happening that way."

As they slosh past the display windows of the appliance section, amid the tires and fan belts and antifreeze cans, Vi sees their reflections, three bundled figures, straggling heavily along in single file.

On the way to the airport, they stop for chowder and clam cakes in the Lobster Shack. "We tried to think of what local delicacies you might not get out there," Nick says. "Of course, you never can tell how good the chowder's going to be. This is a little past its prime, don't you think? See, the potatoes are all crumbling. Last time we were here, they put more clam bits in the cakes."

"Oh, these are fine," Vi says, trying to finish one.

"We could have them pack some in a carton for you to carry back," Sue says.

"No, this one is all I need," Vi says.

She can feel a cloud of tiredness settling over them as they struggle over mounds of gritty snow into the airport. The visit has aged them. They scuff heavily into the steamy waiting room. It seems to be filled with large families, mostly speaking Spanish, clinging, being tender, looking as if they would cry.

"It went so fast, your being here," Sue says. "We should have had a dinner party for you. We should have taken you out more. We were so selfish, wanting to keep you to ourselves."

"Don't worry. It was fine," Vi says.

"You're just saying that to make us feel good. You only saw the four walls. The next time you come, we'll do all the right things, won't we, Nick?"

He nods but stares toward his shoes.

Sue continues, "We could have taken you to that new Chinese restaurant in East Greenwich. If it had been summer, we could have gone to Block Island. We never went to the Mystic Aquarium. Or the Seaport."

Vi interrupts, "Look, it was fine."

Sue says, desperately, "It breaks our hearts. We want to make it up to you. We pray for you all the time."

On the plane she has an aisle seat. She prefers the aisle seat. The couple next to her turn out to be first-time flyers. They want to be noticed. Even before takeoff, their conversation spills beyond their space. They rummage through their seat pockets as if they expect surprises there. She can feel them aching to speak. Finally they come up with a request. Can she turn their matching digital watches to western time?

"Usually," the wife says, "we keep them at standard all year and just add an hour for daylight until we're right again, but we're going to visit our son, and we don't want to let him know that we're afraid of them. He bought these for us in Japan, you know. He travels all over. Do you?"

"Not if I can help it," Vi says.

"Are you going to visit someone," the wife asks.

"No, I've been." That information does not seem to satisfy them, so Vi adds with finality, "I used to live here. I hate to come back. It's like viewing the remains."

"Oh, my," the wife says with a frightened look toward her husband. They will not bother Vi for the rest of the trip and whisper only to each other.

Gypsies

The third summer of the gypsy moth infestation, the year they crashed, was also the season of Tom Madden's affair with Emily and the time when his wife, Gwyn, was dying. All three surreal dramas unfolded in domestic settings but with individual pain. Rooted in habit, Tom survived like grass, far below violent weather.

It took a longer time for events to enter Tom's memory or dreams. There he rejected Gwyn's death. When he thought of her, the pictures were not yet of the hospital but of her fussing with the petunias, or raging in the kitchen, or ranting into the telephone, or stubbing out the morning's first cigarette. He supposed all the frenzy and vitality would fade and there would be bare spots in the tapestry of memory. Already her voice and laugh had dimmed considerably.

It was also the spring he had turned fifty-four and had grown accustomed to being in that decade at all. Almost everyone was younger than he, everywhere he went.

The week after his birthday, Gwyn was returning from a doctor's appointment. As soon as she had left the office, the doctor had called Tom with the bad news about the latest X rays. After the Volvo stopped ferociously in the driveway, he waited for her to slam all the doors and to begin shouting to herself in the kitchen before he walked out and awkwardly put his arms around her. They had not embraced this way for years.

She struggled free and sat down at the kitchen table. "I can't believe it."

"It may not be true," he said.

"It's a death sentence, except no one knows the execution date."

"Don't say that."

"But I'm supposed to, and you are too, on the principle that we'll get used to the word and not turn coward."

"We'll turn it around."

"No use. He's been brutally direct with me."

"What are we supposed to do?"

"According to him, devise strategy. Develop a game plan. They use military metaphors entirely."

"Can't they talk straight?"

"None of them do. It's like keeping tabs on Medusa. You're supposed to use a mirror. Try to catch it off guard."

What the doctor had, quite ponderously, told Tom was that no one could estimate the speed of the metastasis. "She could be maintained for a long period. Some are, but probably not in this instance." So Gwyn sat at the top of the Ferris wheel with the motor idling. She would soon begin the fall from one emergency to another.

For about a month she was still at home between treatments. She gave a last, uncharacteristically elegant dinner party, and he found her being sick in the sink when he came into the kitchen for the coffee cups. They had tickets for the Beaux Arts Quartet, but she could only stay until the first intermission. Evidently, she napped in the afternoons in order to seem rested, but after dinner on a tray while they watched the news, she slowly climbed the stairs and sank into a long, dark sleep. "The medicine is tiring me," she said. "I can't think clearly. I'm being smothered in flannel."

He fluttered around uselessly. "Don't worry," he said stupidly.

"I don't," she answered. "They tell me they'll spare me the worst pain, so there's nothing to fear."

Fortunately, she had left her job in a central city high school several years before, when they no longer needed the extra income. She had not enjoyed it, had cursed the dumb regulations and silly forms, had worried about the drugs and faculty burnout. Police patrolled the corridors, and the principal hid out in his office, occasionally shouting over the PA.

Tom thought that fate had crossed its computer wires. He had assumed that he would die first. His own father had keeled over at fifty behind the wheel in a rest area off Route 93, but his mother at seventy-two was still trying on bathing suits in Fort Lauderdale.

He heard Gwyn saying goodbye to trees and plants in the garden. She took gardening too seriously to talk about it with anyone. Her rages at him, her tantrums and arguments with almost everyone she had ever known, were calmed by trees and flowers. They lived in a wreck of a house that had been her mother's summer place, surrounded by splendid trees and ambitious gardens. She had planted ceremonial trees for birthdays and anniversaries, living Christmas trees, rosebushes for stages in their son's life, little shrubs to mark other events. He had grown up in an apartment in the Bronx. He appreciated grand vistas but could not enjoy rearranging small sections of nature. Gardening seemed to him a futile struggle. Decay and pests were always chewing and spoiling: aphids, weevils, cabbage worms, Japanese beetles, finally the frost itself. But he tried to remember to water what he thought were flowers.

In late May the trees were overtaken by an infestation of millions of dexterous caterpillars, dangerously energetic. The lava advanced steadily up the trunks of every tree like two-inch-long furry bags. Then they flung themselves down on almost invisible silken strands toward the ground to denude another plant. Off went all the leaves and needles. This was the peak year of the gypsy moth epidemic.

Lying alone in his big bed, Tom heard them eat their five pounds of leaves through the day and night. He was wrong. The noise was not their jaws but the sound of their excrement dropping. It fell in lacy brown fragments and bright green flecks over the grass and cars and road.

With the leaves and needles gone, it looked like winter by mid-June. The ghostly trees stood in the summer sun. Squashed under foot, the caterpillars were blobs of brown and green. Their soft, hairy bodies plopped onto faces and hair. Finally, on the silent brown tips of trees, they were overtaken by the pupa stage. After another week, the air would be full of dense tan wings, the males flying desperately toward the scent of the heavy females, pressing blindly over window screens, feathering human faces. Finally, when the whole ritual was over, light brown egg masses promising millions more lava for the next summer would be stuck high on the trunks and branches.

"No two cases follow the same pattern," the surgeon said unnecessarily. Gwyn had not lived by any perceptible pattern. She wore summer clothes most of the year because she preferred them, Indian
dresses because she liked the feel of cotton, long, full skirts that
slapped around her bare legs. Even now in the hospital, she had wound
a batik scarf over her thin hair. Her sandals were under the bed in case
she felt strong enough. She smoked five cigarettes a day, always when
someone was present in the room, in case she fell asleep.

Because he saw her every day, the changes in her face were less
shocking to Tom than weekly visitors found them. Surprise and pain hit
their expressions at the door of the room before they adjusted to the
newest loss. Gwyn dozed unpredictably during their conversations but
seldom awakened refreshed from the naps. As her eyes opened reluctantly, she murmured out of the last scene of the nightmare, "I tried to
save them. I called out to all of them, but some of them are still back in
that building. They'll be burned to death. Do something about it. I
don't have the strength," she whispered to him. For a week she had
been barely escaping from burning warehouses or from collapsing
bridges or running from the cone of the tornado. Her clawed hand
groped for his. "Do something. Help me save them."

It was in his evening class that he met Emily. It was university policy
that everyone taught one night course every third semester. So that
spring it was his turn. There were thirty students when the course
began and, of course, several of them would disappear, not always the
predictable ones. The future drop-outs would arrive ten or fifteen minutes late and sit there restlessly thinking about what they were missing
on TV. The way they shut the door on their last night indicated that
they wouldn't be back. There were also a few well-known crazies who
seemed to have no daytime life. They never dropped.

Tom thought that there was something poignant about the tired men
in business suits and the women in eye makeup and high heels arguing
intensely about whether Daisy Miller was indiscreet in not getting into
the carriage with Winterbourne or whether Hester Prynne only felt
sorry for Dimmesdale. They wanted to know if Whitman was a Christian and why Emily Dickinson didn't marry and whether Cummings
was on drugs and if Thoreau was a mental case.

Sometimes their energetic forays into intentions and ideas tired him. He had long ago given up taking literature seriously, and Gwyn's decay was gnawing at him. One night in class a young black woman became hysterical during a discussion about Faulkner's Dilsey. Weeping, she accused the class of patronizing her. Several members of the class tried to embrace her. She screamed that she would not be touched. Someone trained in therapy demanded that they all breathe deeply and meditate for five minutes. It was only nine o'clock with an hour to go, but Tom dismissed them. They would not leave. Only he slunk out the door. He felt fragile and inept. He dreaded the next meeting, practiced calm opening statements.

By the next week they had forgotten the whole episode. When he asked rhetorical questions, they waved their arms in the air. They were treasuries of irrelevant but curious experiences. They wore him out. And he was sure that they had a low opinion of his clothes and hang-dog look.

What did they have to do with him and his current vigil, anyway? He tried to forget them from one week to the next. It was messy getting involved with one's students. Several bad examples lurked in his recent memory. A sententious composition instructor had fallen head over heels for a disorderly boy in her remedial class and had left her husband and children for him. Of course, the boy promptly threw her over when he realized that she wouldn't supply his drug habit and by then her husband wouldn't take her back. During her breakdown, she ran out of sick leave. The man in the next office to Tom scheduled evening conferences and locked the door. He had a reclining chair, allegedly for his bad back. He was a marrier. So far, he had married and divorced three girl-wives, each younger, creating a tangle of children and houses. At his last wedding reception, he had stood wearily beside Tom, his best man, and muttered, "It would be nice if this one could last."

The evening division was located in a remodeled shoe factory in an industrial park. It was convenient to the interstate, had abundant parking, and had been a bargain. From the windows of his third-floor classroom, Tom looked at a glowing Midas muffler sign and a solemn blue neon cross on an evangelical church. The blue-black spring night was heavy with a burning smell from a pasta factory. On the other side of the building, on the interstate, trucks thundered by and occasional ambulances and fire trucks. At half way through the three-hour class, there was supposed to be a ten-minute break. A quilted steel panel truck, "Iggy's Hot Stop," parked outside and served pizza, coffee, and hero sandwiches. All around the truck stood clumps of coffee drinkers at a sort of half-hearted picnic.

Tom leaned out of the window and stared down at his students. He was ashamed that he could not recognize most of them. One of them looked up and, seeing him, called up in a clear voice, "Come down. Join us."

"All right. I'll be down," he shouted. The young woman, Emily, who had called out, handed him a cup of coffee. That was how it began. He was vulnerable, and it probably showed.

"It was my fault," he told her, a month later as he drove her home after the last class.

"Why does it have to be anyone's fault?" she asked. "You want everything clearly defined. It happened, that's all."

She was the age of his son, twenty-eight. Except when questioned, she did not talk much about her past, and Tom was unable or unwilling to find out any information beyond what she volunteered. Sometimes when he telephoned her in the evenings, she spoke guardedly, and he knew she was not alone. Her life seemed more temporary and accidental than he could imagine. Her mother, who lived in Cleveland, telephoned her fairly often, and he presumed that she sent money. Emily had dropped out of art school long before, when she discovered that she would never be a real painter. Now she was a potter and she sold everything she made. She priced her mugs and casseroles modestly, and she told him that she deliberately produced objects that would sell. They were almost as ordinary and dependable as mass produced, but prettier. "I'm simply practical," she said. "When it's time and when I'm ready, I'll make good stuff."

She seemed to have all the time in the world. She was tall and large boned. Tom could not figure out how she had happened to him. When he had courted Gwyn, they had driven each other crazy with scenes and demands and promises and ultimatums and reconciliations. Both of them had cried and ranted and trembled, apart and together. They had written ten-page letters and handed them to each other. They had sat on park benches in the rain and on cold stone steps, telling and explaining. Whatever this relationship with Em was, it had different weather and pace. It was bounded by their slow, wordless embracing. He loved the smell of her skin and slept with his nose pressed against her fleshy back.

He was dismayed when he saw her handwriting. Her two papers for the course had been typed and proofed by someone else. Then she left a scribbled note under the windshield wiper, and he could not understand what it said. "Your handwriting isn't quite what I expected," he said lamely.

"It's terrible, isn't it? I can't spell either. Does that bother you?"

"I'm sorry, but it does. I ought to be above all that."

"I guessed it would," she shrugged. "We really don't know much about each other, do we? I suppose you know everything about Gwyn."

He thought he did. He told Emily, "It flattens time, dying does."

"What's that supposed to mean?"

"The past and the now are jammed together. There aren't any lines between." He was too tired to explain properly. What he had noticed was that Gwyn had become attached to all sorts of comforters, the whole hospital Mafia: technicians, therapists, aides, and specialists.

Women she had worked with made picnic excursions to her room. He felt the stranger. "Oh, Tom," she would say. "Look who's here. Do you remember Mabel and Fran? And this is Aunt Helen's daughter." They would giggle together, talking nonsense.

When they left he said, "I never get a chance to be alone with you."

"I'm not very good company," she said. But as the malignancy chewed deeper, she became indiscriminate. It did not matter who the guests were as long as they stayed. At this stage, she did not want to be alone.

It grew harder to face her face. Some new destruction, new smell, new hurt every day. He prepared himself by walking up the two flights instead of taking the elevator.

"She'll be less bright with this medication," the surgeon advised. "That's a side effect. Also the deafness."

So, coming into her room unheard, he caught her off guard. She was staring at her hand, which was fluttering. "Well, I'm certainly a mess.

My hands are like claws and on top of everything else, they move independently. There seems to be some private motor down there."

"We need to talk," he said on one bad afternoon.

"Do we really? I don't think so. I don't have to do anything now."

"But, Gwyn, I have to explain things."

"Oh, let's not get into those ultimate statements. Let's keep it light."

The nurse came to give her a shot. Even as Tom encouraged a serious talk, he was afraid that she might make some ruthless final statement: "I wasted my life." "You made me a miserable woman." But that did not happen. She became more tender, especially with strangers. An aide with splotchy skin and dirty hair, who seemed a little dull witted, bent over Gwyn and then told him, "I love this here lady. I never seen her before last week, but I really love her."

The surgeon carefully explained the palliative operation, using the back of a get-well card to draw a cross section of the muscles. "We cut through this mass, like so. She will feel a little discomfort from the incision, but she may get a few weeks of relief. She's agreed, and we wanted you to understand."

Tom thanked him.

"And how are you getting on yourself?" the surgeon asked. "Don't be afraid to ask for help. Would you like to see someone?"

"What do you mean?"

"Now don't get spooked. We have a therapist on call—someone to talk about problems you're having in sleeping or coping day by day."

"I wouldn't know where to begin," Tom said. "Right now, sorting things out would be too much trouble to make it worthwhile."

The real problem right then was with the house. All at once, it was calling attention to itself, falling apart, or sections of it were. There was mold on the kitchen wall. The toilets gurgled. Groating seeped from the shower tiles. The garage door stuck, half way up. Someone stole the mail box. Squirrels were in the drains. Then there were the bills and the checkbook mess and endless forms from medical insurance, doctors, the hospital. The forms made no sense. He could not separate those that needed response from copies of payments already made. Coming back from visiting the hospital at night, he sometimes didn't turn on the first-floor lights but went upstairs, feeling his way in the dark to avoid the disorder.

Everywhere he went, listing piles of papers accused him. Old students whose faces he couldn't remember called apologetically about missing recommendations they had needed weeks before. "I hate to bother you. I know that this is an awful time for you. I wouldn't ask, except . . ."

Every mail put him further behind. And then the box got stolen. The motherly departmental secretary called out, "If there's anything I can do, just let me know." So did almost everyone he met. He felt breakable. He was treated with caution, even avoided.

His nightly visits to Gwyn were now penance, putting in time. Heavy footed, he dragged himself down the third-floor corridor toward her room, torpor and sickness settling over him. His shoulders pulled down his neck. Catching a glimpse of himself in her bathroom mirror, he was shocked by his angry face.

Dying provided another climate entirely. The flowers and plants that arrived fresh melted immediately in the heat of the room. The rose buds blackened before they had a chance to open.

Gwyn lay in the half-dark room watching TV. At least the set was on, but the sound was turned down. Her eyes were half open. The remote control button had slipped from her hand. Tom watched the dumb show of some kind of drug bust in city housing, a bunch of young men in tight jeans filing out of the crumbling doorway and putting their jackets over their heads as they passed the cameras. Then some kids in wheelchairs and braces pursed their contorted faces to cross the finish line in a special Olympics.

He turned up the sound for the month's continuing big story, the caterpillar invasion. Angry men hosed off their cars. Children showed their swollen arms. Their irate mother scolded, "I don't care what the health department says. They got a rash off them worms. We've been sick to our stomachs since May. What I want to know is what the guys in the state house are going to do about this crazy business."

The moth spraying controversy had exploded. The Audubon Society president cited the dangers to bluebirds and bees. Helicopters took off at dawn to spray with Sevin and Dylox, trying to avoid the houses with NO SPRAY flags. The state was a patchwork of townships, some supporting aerial spraying, some donating fifty dollars to any household that hired ground sprayers. The TV camera panned over moth traps and burlap strips and aluminum rings and whitewashed tree trunks. In the next sequence an angry objector to spraying was demonstrating vandalism to her house by prospraying advocates. Tom recognized her face: she was always on the side of liberal causes—for the bottle bill, on the side of battered women and grey whales, against Christmas creches in public buildings. Patiently she demonstrated the hole in her shattered solar panel and the brick thrown through it. "Crap. That's crap. I hope they eat her alive," a thickset man in a Spray 'Em Dead T-shirt shouted in the next sequence.

Finally Tom saw his colleague Flash Brindle standing in his entomology lab. Flash was painfully shy, rumored to be close only to spiders and his aging sister, Olga. He smiled nervously while describing the capacity of male moths to follow the trail of the odor plume emitted by the female moths. The newsman interrupted Flash impatiently in mid sentence, "What Dr. Brindle means is True Love finds a way. Neither wind nor rain will stop them, but cheer up, folks, this is the year they crash."

Gwyn's eyes had closed, and she slept heavily. She began to snore lightly. Before he left, he kissed her forehead and stroked her thin arm.

He drove the car into the garage through veils of tan gypsy moths. He wanted to be near the phone in case Gwyn might call him. Sometimes he was able to talk her back to sleep if she had a bad spot in the middle of the night. They were always easy on the telephone with the protection of distance between them but especially now that he could forget what had happened to her.

Emily had promised to stop by and to help him straighten up some of the clutter. He vacuumed all the rugs and threw out the junk mail. When Emily came, she went to work on the refrigerator. She moved around economically, not making much noise. She had never been in the house before, but she seemed to have a sense of where dishes would go and what needed to be thrown away. He watched her from a distance. She had just washed her long, thick hair and had pulled it loosely back to dry.

She turned and said, "All right. Enough of this. Can we go to bed now?"

They used the guest room, of course. He would have insisted on that, even if Emily had not asked first. The whole performance embarrassed him. He wondered if she had offered herself for his sake.

"No, I'm no therapist," she said. "And I'm not a habit-forming drug, either. Still, it's better than talk, isn't it. Do you want to talk?"

"I do, Emily. It's unfair, but I do."

She sighed. "Most things are unfair. Go ahead. Talk then."

He shut his eyes, wondering how to begin.

She stretched her body, turned on her side, one arm elbowed and touched his cheek. "All right. Let's not talk. What to say anyway? You'd regret saying it later, and I'd remember too much. The cure is in not letting yourself remember too much."

She got up and began to dress, "I'll make us some dinner."

"We could go out."

"No. You can't go out to dinner with another woman while your wife is dying in Hillcrest." So she drove away and brought back spare ribs, and they ate them on paper plates in the living room.

Tom jumped when the telephone rang, but it was not Gwyn. It was their son, who called every few days from Houston. He was a computer programmer living in a singles condo, already divorced from the girl he had married in college. When Gwyn was first diagnosed, he had come and sat silently around with them for one long weekend, and he had made another trip when the doctor said she was at a crisis point.

"I hate to admit this, Dad," he said, "but I'm not good at saying goodbye over and over. I feel like hell about it, but there's not a damned thing I can do. I can't think of things to tell her. We never really had a serious conversation before, and we can't start now. Every time I telephone the hospital, she's sleeping or having a test. Maybe I want it that way. I'm going to come at the end."

"Nobody knows when the end will be."

"Sure. I realize that. It's all one long end every day, I guess."

"Thanks for calling. Take care of yourself," Tom said.

In the living room, Emily was watching a PBS special on dolphins that had been taught to recognize picture signs for frisbees and beach balls and then to press buttons.

"Over-achievers," she said. "For a couple of fish, they'll learn a new word."

"They look happy," Tom observed.

"Why does a dolphin need to chat about beach balls? Are they better off for having a two-hundred-word vocabulary?"

"I sometimes wonder too," Tom said. "All this endless improving.

Like forcing firemen and cashiers to read John of the Cross and *Walden.*"

"Keeps you employed. Pays for all of this."

"I suppose. I'm certainly asking all the cosmic questions."

"There may be questions, but there sure aren't any answers. Try to avoid harming people if you can. That's my only rule. Be glad to put your feet down on the floor every morning."

"What are you going to do finally, Emily?"

"You mean when I grow up? God, Tom, look at me. I'm twenty-eight. I'm what I'm going to be."

"I mean—marriage, kids?"

"Probably not. I told you before. I lived five years with one man once. Supermarried routine: Thanksgiving turkey with the stuffing, Christmas tree. Written contract even: costs shared right down the middle, who went to the laundromat when. You know, a week after we split, it was as if I'd never been there. Another woman moved into the place. I've been over for sauerbraten with them. He's a dynamite cook and a fiend about cleanliness. She is too. She may last longer than I did."

"Don't you get lonely?"

"Terribly. Why do you think I'm here? Nothing fills the want. Excuse me, but not even you. Especially not you. But I'm a sprinter, not a long-distance runner. I'm doing all right now. It's going to get harder later."

"I suppose you think I'm taking advantage of you."

"No more than I'm taking advantage of you. It's not very elegant, but I believe we were put here to use each other, up to a point, all of us."

Tom groaned, "It's so damned hard, watching Gwyn slip. Every day another indignity."

"Maybe you ought not to go every night. Sometimes she's not even awake."

"I can explain," he said. "I'm serving time. I am paying."

"Paying for what?"

"For love. For the past. Just paying."

"So." She got up. "I've got to go now. I'll call you."

But she didn't.

Gwyn's decline accelerated. The process of her dying was both tranquil and deliberate. She was moved to another, quieter wing of the hospital, where the emphasis was on last comforts. The wing was furnished casually, with donations from the houses of those recently dead. There were velvet settees and wing chairs and a glass-topped metal table with matching white iron chairs from someone's patio. All of this was the domain of Max, the interdenominational chaplain.

Gwyn had been a cradle Catholic with one great uncle who became a monsignor. She had attended parochial gradeschool and continued to go to mass for years, long after she lost her faith. They had been married in a city hall during the lunch hour. She told Tom, "I want us to start out fairly. If we need five bridesmaids in pink organdy and a Papal blessing to stick us together, something's wrong."

Now Max had become her closest friend. He was a sad gnome with full white beard, who squished from room to room on crepe soles. Sometimes Gwyn asked Tom to leave her room while she and Max whispered together. Tom could not understand what they could have in common, and Max did not give reports.

"How are you doing?" He slid down beside Tom on the settee in the conversation area. "Are you eating all right? You need to keep up your strength."

Tom stared at him. It was July and vacation, and he was spending most of the days at the hospital. He had taken up smoking again, and his mouth was sour from continuous coffee. When he got home, he sometimes opened a can and ate the cold contents directly.

Max said, "I'd invite you home, but the truth is my wife is a terrible cook. Every meal is a crisis. So I eat here in the cafeteria. Let's go down together."

Over the gelid remains of roast pork, mashed potato, and apple sauce, Tom looked across at Max searching through the numerous pockets of his rumpled corduroy jacket. Finally, he pulled out two rings, "You'll want to put these away. Her fingers are so thin, they fell off." They were Gwyn's wedding and engagement rings. Max fished into another pocket and produced a rather elegant fountain pen and a little leather book in which he found a page, which Tom could see was marked "Gwyn." "What I thought is that we'd talk a little about the service. We've sort of worked it out, she and I. Very simple and

direct—you know, Corinthians 13 and a touch of Ecclesiastes—
Dignified stuff. Maybe you'd like to suggest something secular—
Dickinson or Frost, something down your line. And we've picked out
three tight hymns."

"Tight hymns?"

"Not the kind that give crying fits. We don't want people collapsing,
you know."

When he got home, as he was showering, it came to him that the
gypsy moths had disappeared. The late TV news was concentrating on
new horrors—the Mediterranean fruit fly and the tent caterpillars.
Something was eating the white pines. A volcanic cloud had dimmed
the sun's rays and was changing the weather.

Max telephoned him at three a.m. to say that Gwyn had just died.

Late August was the season of fairs and crafts shows in the city's
parks and shopping malls. Like gypsies turned capitalists, the weavers
and leather workers and potters traveled from fair to fair, their vans full
of the winter's production—jewelry, polished stones, stained glass,
leather belts and bags, mobiles and treasure boxes, batik and paintings.

The Westlake Mall had become a busy little village, all the craftsmen
playing street merchants in front of Woolworth's and Thom McAn.
Saturday shoppers and senior citizens from the nearby high rises were
confused by the dislocation.

Emily unfolded a card table, covered it with an Indian woven spread,
unpacked and arranged her pots, put up her beach umbrella, and settled
onto a webbed chair with a copy of *Moby Dick*.

Coming up from the parking lot behind Sears, Tom took a few minutes to spot her, stretched out on her webbed deck chair, reading a
thick book. He had not seen her in almost two months. She seemed not
to notice the people touching and lifting her bowls and mugs. She had
told him that at first she hated this part of the business but had learned
to ignore the canned hurdy-gurdy music swirling over the plaza and the
uncomfortable chatter going on over her wares.

He groped for a clever greeting, but none came. "Hi. How are you?"
He had to repeat the Hi before she lifted her head.

"Oh, Tom," she said. "I wondered if you'd have the courage to come
over. Glad you did."

"You saw me before? Did I look ridiculous?"

"My God. Is that what you worry about? No, you looked fine. Just near sighted."

"How are you really doing?" he asked again.

"Fine. Don't I look fine? But how are you coping?"

"Getting better gradually." He looked at her pottery.

She handed him a small jar. "Here's one for you. First quality." And when she saw him fumbling for his wallet, she said, "No. It's a gift, a souvenir. It's for honey."

A young man with pale blue eyes and neat beard came up behind her and laid his hand on her shoulder. She introduced him to Tom. "Sean's a glass blower. We're doing the craft fairs in his van. Lucky for me."

"Yes, it is," Tom said. "I hope you do well. Both of you. Thanks for the jar. It's beautiful."

When he got home, he mowed the side yard. As he was admiring the results, he realized that there were shadows again. He looked up at the small green plumes on every oak branch. The trees were struggling to leaf once more. It was a second spring just before September. There were almost no egg masses. The caterpillars had crashed.

A Private Space

A man, a human being, Sid tells himself, has a right to some privacy. No matter how old or dumb or how long married, he has the right to at least a shelf all his own.

The biggest mystery to Sid Crane is how he has suddenly gotten old and invisible to everybody but his wife, Cleo. He would like to get some opportunities back. He would like to dance again with Skipper Tralee, a girl in a red sweater that he met at the USO in Portland on his way back from Saipan. All night, while they were doing the Lindy, Skipper was describing her horse—its markings, mane, leg action, flanks. He never saw her again.

Before the war he had a job as a grease monkey at the Socony station at the corner of Elm. Worked in the pit all day. Was going steady with Alice Kowalski. But she got tired of writing V-Letters and married Bob something-or-other, had twins, and went to flesh.

When he got back from the Pacific, his mom was dead, and he was almost thirty. He used his bonus to lease the Socony station, which had an apartment over the garage. Trucks wanting gas in the middle of the night tripped a cord that set off a bell. Route 1 went right through the center of town then. He slept in his clothes and read when he awakened. Got a library card and bought up years of the Geographic at auctions. Listened to the Texaco opera on Saturdays.

Before he retired, he owned a big station, forty pumps open twenty-four hours, on the new interstate north of town. But he preferred the place on Elm. Dreams a lot about that apartment, how he could remodel it. Put in a good FM radio and a nice nineteen-inch color TV and get "Nova" and "Masterpiece Theatre." Rig up a fireplace, put up some Japanese prints. Of course, they bulldozed the garage twenty years back for municipal parking. Most everybody he knew then has kicked the bucket—all dead as doornails.

His mother had sized him up perfectly. "You're too tender hearted. You won't get anywhere that way." By the time he knew how right she was, he'd gotten roped into marrying Cleo. It might have been worse. Cleo'd been passed over, like him. But she was a lady, had all the credentials: college diploma, fair skin, family tree practically back to Noah, real gold bracelets around her thin wrists, and a 1940 Packard Clipper that had belonged to her dad.

The Packard brought them together, as she put it. The ignition went on the fritz in bad weather, even with only the threat of rain. She would ring him at ten of eight, despair just behind her voice, apologizing for the bother. She let him know she'd already been sitting in the car for an hour, leaving enough time between starting attempts to prevent flooding, as he'd taught her.

Sid guesses that thousands of marriages begin this way, a scared woman late for work bending over a dead engine. A competent mechanic drives up, attaches the jump cables, and saves the day. It isn't a love affair but a marriage. Amid the acrid exhaust fumes they stare down the years. Even through her thick glasses, she can see the future better than he: she is a few years older.

He wonders how she looks at life, but she cuts short that topic. "Cleo, what is it all about? How did we get here? What joker planned this carnival anyway?"

"I don't know what you're talking about," she says, when she does answer. "You could be handicapped. You could be in Africa."

Once he looked up the definition of irony, and he realizes that it is not in the dictionary but right there in their marriage. He always worries about the wrong things. At first his biggest worry in the marriage was not being smart enough. There he was, a high school drop-out, a mechanic, marrying a college graduate with a fancy name—Cleo La-Salle. Huguenots, they called themselves, to differentiate from French Canadians. Then he learned that the LaSalles were poorer than church mice, and the college she had gone to was only a sort of finishing school. Her family was, she said, "cultured." That meant they used cloth napkins; had nice penmanship, good posture, and small noses and mouths; did not swear in public; wore hats and gloves and worried about their underwear. Her posture is still good. He sees her straighten up in front of mirrors and stick out her chin. If only she had liked him more, he might have loved her.

They used to say you could look at your mother-in-law and see how your wife would look finally. He first saw Mrs. LaSalle when she was almost seventy. If he looks hard at Cleo now, he sees a carbon copy, not that anyone uses carbon paper any more. He thought Mrs. LaSalle would never die, but she did. He thought that he was fairly successful with old people until he became one. He called his mother-in-law Mrs. LaSalle, not mother or Jessie, for which she gave permission. Kept her supplied with licorice and cigarettes. Stayed with her while she smoked one cigarette after dinner and aired the room so that Cleo would not discover. "Our little secret," Mrs. LaSalle wheezed. "You're a good provider, Sidney. You were well brought up. You've come a long way."

Now he and Cleo live in Golden Manor. In the basement each family has a little storage space, a thin, deep closet, probably five-by-fifteen feet, where they can keep what they can't bear to part with—the best china, mama's fur coat, somebody's mandolin, the cuckoo clock. Not that the building super approves. "What you need is a good up and out," he says. "One good up and out. Right into the Goodwill box." Everything in their basement storage is from the LaSalles. When both of them are gone, the super will cart out their treasures and chuck them into the dumpster. Fringe from Mrs. LaSalle's mothy pink shawl will hang over the side.

Cleo appropriates. She took back for herself the cardigan sweater she'd given him last Christmas, and she wears his striped flannel pajamas. She is not being coy or mean. She simply wants them. Fingering the neat collar of the cardigan, she says, "I don't know why they waste such quality on men's clothing."

He does not tell her that he is probably more interested in textures and colors than she is. She does not know that he roams the clothes racks in St. Vincent's to look at the old Harris tweed jackets and Pendleton shirts. If he had somewhere to hide it, he would buy the moss-green plaid shirt he tried on one day. It had a few burn holes and a chipped button. But she would put him through the third degree. "Throw it out. No telling what infection you can pick up from rags."

"You're always trying to walk out on me," she says. "I can feel you plotting escape. Any other man would be happy to spend the afternoon sensibly at home." Most of the few men left at Golden Manor can't be trusted alone, anyway. Might set fire to the chair. Unplug the Frigidaire. Wander downstreet. Take all the money out of the joint savings account in cash, and then slide the bills into a trash can.

"What's funny?" Cleo asks.

"Nothing," he replies.

"You were smiling just then." She keeps tabs. "Are you going out again? You've already been out once today. Well, I'm glad I went downtown yesterday."

"To the hairdressing academy?" he asks.

She doesn't like to be reminded that the students work on the elderly for half price. "They are gaining experience. I am advancing their education."

He stares at her head, which always looks the same. "How?" he asks.

Encouraged, she says airily, "Everything can be told from the hair: pregnancy, anxiety, diet, depression. Of course, you have no secrets there." He has been bald for a long time.

He is already struggling into his coat. He would like to hurl some grand revelation over his shoulder, but he simply lets the door slam like an exclamation point.

He is in luck; he has timed it perfectly. The bus is waiting. He hoists himself up its steps and collapses into the front seat, careful not to show that he is puffing. He flashes his senior permit, but the driver hardly looks. Anyone boarding there has to be old.

Sid does have a secret. A month ago he rented his own box for mail at the annex post office, clear over on the other side of town. As a precaution he rented the middle-sized box, just in case it fills up before he is able to get there. Mail needs nudging, so he sent away for a few catalogs to get his name on lists. Of course, he receives no real letters, but he likes the sweepstakes invitations, customized to the Sidney Cranes of Box 85 for the vacation home of their dreams or the matching Mercedes. He studies the photographs of successful winners accepting their checks and then he carefully follows the complicated rules.

The atmosphere of the annex P.O. is brisk and happy. Lots of young people, students, have boxes, especially if they are conducting romances by mail. They run in, trailing hair, scarves, long skirts, and sandals, smelling of the wind, their faces lovely, their full lips slightly open to show their strong white teeth. Sid takes a certain pleasure in realizing that all of them will be alive when he is dead. Not only will they be alive, but they will be rushing through all the thousand little pleasures and big disappointments he knows all about. They'll stand at the mirror one day and see the first white hairs and the wrinkles starting. Finally, they'll wind up invisible too.

He enjoys the bus ride. It is the longest ride in the city, an hour each way from Golden Manor across town to the university and back again, the driver sitting fifteen minutes at each end before starting up. It circles into a shopping mall which always has something going on: bits and pieces of a circus, a boy who juggles and rides a unicycle, a girl in white face and a black suit who acts out little stories.

The bus ride frames his life. He can see himself dimly reflected in store windows as they pass: a man with a respectable hat and face going some place where he is expected. A lot of women ride the bus. Sid likes their company. He thinks, on the whole, that women age better than men. Sometimes he strikes up conversations with them, especially the ones who pick up their children from the nursery near the university at the end of the day. They are headed home, their feet killing them, their kids restless, their faces troubled about what they will cook for dinner. Sometimes one of the younger children will lean against Sid. Beneath the soft jacket, he can feel the small bones. "Look," Sid will tell the child as he clasps his hands shut, the index fingers out, touching. "Here's the church, and here's the steeple," and then, reversing his hands. "See. Here are the people." Most of the children are suspicious, but their mothers often smile at him.

This afternoon, as they climb the hill toward the university, the passengers thin out considerably. The driver looks across at Sid as if to remind him to get off at the last stop. He lets himself down stiffly and is careful with the wet leaves on the pavement.

Someone holds the door of the post office open for him. Box 85 is conveniently at eye level. And surprisingly there is something in it that looks like a real letter. He takes it out, shuts the little door, and walks over to the windows where the light is better. He doesn't recognize the handwriting. It isn't really writing but block printing with a thick black nib and no return address. He pries open the flap. There is just one sheet with a few lines block printed in the center.

SIDNEY CRANE———
YOU SNEAK. KNOW ALL ABOUT YOU.
OUT CHASING WOMEN. YOU CANT HIDE.
GOT YOUR NUMBER. WATCH YOUR STEP.

It isn't signed, of course. His hands are shaking with fear and anger. His knees are weak. He wishes he could sit down somewhere. Leaning over the slanting desk and hiding the sheet a little, he read the words again, but they won't change.

It has to be Cleo. Who else cares enough? Somehow she has found out about his box and is taking that over too. He looks again at the envelope, postmarked the day before, mailed from downtown when she went to the hairdressing academy.

He would like longer to figure out what to do, but he doesn't want to miss the return bus. He will try to pretend that the letter hasn't arrived. He puts it back in the envelope, which he tears into pieces and throws into the wastepaper basket. Then he walks cautiously toward the waiting bus.

The Woman Who
Would Not Stay Home

For some the first memory is a pony's wet muzzle finding the sugar cube, an arm socket being pulled as some out-of-sight giant snatches one's hand, a design on the bedroom wallpaper, the poor burned foot under the spilled hot water amid the shouts, "I told you! I warned you!" Loretta Huff's first memory was all motion: the loose sway of the yellow trolley, green branches coming in the windows, the backs of her knees pricked by the shellacked straw seat. Her mother is only a plaid rayon skirt. Ret flinches a little at the branches, but otherwise she stares steadily ahead at the conductor's cap in the center of the narrowing green tunnel until they reach the river and then race the water itself, black water carrying scraps of wood, old tires. She holds the token, with its cutout design she can already recognize, until it is time to put it into the conductor's hand. Her mother's voice goes on and on.

At four she is taken by bus to kindergarten. The steps are high but she pulls herself up and falls into the seat behind the driver, her legs stretched out from the warm leather settee. In her fierce fist is clasped the red circus car box of animal crackers. The driver smokes a big cigar and shouts at the big boys in the back. "I can see you. You'll walk home if you do that again." The boys make faces back at him. Since she can not yet read and there are many buses in front of the school, she is supposed to look for Donald Duck's picture on the windshield. When it is not there one day, she rides all afternoon through

strange country. She will not tell them who she is, until her father
comes to pick her up at the dispatcher's office. "She'll go anywhere on
wheels."

In fifth grade, Loretta, in plaid pleated dress made over from her
mother's best skirt, goes on a school trip to Rocky Point. It is June and
they ride on a real bus with the two nuns up front in the first seat. The
windows are open. The hot plush seat itches. Her silk socks creep
down and her lacquered curls escape their still shells. Hurdy-gurdy
music and barkers fight for the air. Loretta touches the dollar bill in her
pocket. "Spend carefully," her father told her. She puts the money on
the roller coaster (five rides), dodge 'em cars (three rides), a candied
apple, a hot dog, and some spun sugar. Cecile LeBeuf and Jimmy
Pepin go into the Tunnel of Love. The nuns wait for them at the exit.
Jimmy's face is covered with Cecile's lipstick. The nuns pull them
apart.

Loretta puts her last nickel in the fortune-telling machine. Inside the
glass cubicle a stuffed gypsy woman bends over some playing cards in
a dumb show. A slip of paper shoots out: "You will go far." Loretta
takes a last ride on the roller coaster and throws up as they get into the
bus. Her dress is wrinkled and stained, but she is still grinning. "What
did you expect? You got over tired," says her mother.

The CYO holds three bake sales and five car washes and sells three
hundred pounds of stale chocolate bars to pay for the overnight trip to
New York. She pretends that she has been on many trains before, but
she runs through all the cars opening the heavy doors and waiting for
them to thunk shut. The conductor shouts, "Take it easy. Slow down.
Where do you think you're going?" The other kids are reading comic
books. She sits in the smoking section then goes into the dining car.
She orders coffee, which she does not like, and she holds the paper
cup, pretending that she is bored, staring sadly out at the dark brick
buildings. "You look like a sick cat," her best friend says. In the city,
they ride up and down on the hotel elevators, lock themselves out of
their room, smell the little cakes of hotel soap, hide from their frantic
chaperon. They stand in line in the snow at Radio City and spend all
their change at the Automat, positioning their glasses under the milk
spigot and watching the sandwiches in the glass boxes move toward

them. As Loretta stands on tiptoe reaching for a subway strap, she feels a hand touching her thigh but does not call out or tell anyone about it. She watches a funny-faced man picking a black banana peel out of a gutter. She sees words she has only heard in the playground spelled out on the walls of buildings they pass. On the return train trip, while the others sleep, she stands on the platform smelling the rank odor rising from the tracks and feeling the vibrating wheels through the floor. She has a headache for three days afterward. She is high strung, they say. It is worth it, and she has a notebook full of her own impressions.

At eighteen Loretta is sitting in a bright orange office with twenty other girls, all selling princess phones on time to welfare families. The girls are always celebrating something: engagements, babies, the end of Lent, Valentine's Day, anniversaries. Loretta thinks most about summer vacation. All winter she collects brochures from a travel agent and looks at pictures of palm trees, stockyards, New Orleans, the Rainbow Room. Her best friend, Evelyn, at the next desk, has gone with her to Rye Beach, to the Pennsylvania Dutch country, and to Washington, D.C.

They are not devout, but they take an excursion pilgrimage to Quebec because it is a good value, long and cheap. Except for one husband and a priest, only women are on the dinky old bus, chugging up the pine-covered mountains in a cloud of exhaust fumes. At Saint Anne de Beaupre they stay, dormitory style, in a brown hotel: linoleum, walls, wicker furniture—all brown. Winter is waiting to take over their room. Eight women unlace their pink corsets slowly, showing chunky thighs, exploding in varicose veins. They change their bunion pads and take milk of magnesia. They wipe their forks with their clean linen handkerchiefs before they begin to eat. They also wipe the toilet seats before sitting.

A fat priest smiles too much at Ret when she buys medals. Everything smells of burned roast and chicory. She sits on the porch and writes big on the post cards, hoping that they will reach home before she does. She goes into the basilica and touches the crutches, braces, canes, and even an old truss strapped to the columns. A crazy man, whose family hopes for his cure, has been left in the basement of the

Redemptorist monastery. Through the bars he sticks his tongue out at her and then thumbs his nose. She turns her back.

The best part is the nightly candlelight procession up the terraced hill past life-sized Stations of the Cross. Flickering tapers illuminate bronze Roman soldiers holding whips, Jews spitting, Pilate sneering, the tired backs of the women gathered under the cross. Ret weeps at her own goodness, imagines herself a barefoot pilgrim on a crusade, but before that will be the return bus trip through Quebec (lunch stop), the eastern townships (tea and souvenir shopping), and overnight in Portland, Maine.

Evelyn will not kiss the relic case, for fear of germs, or climb the Scala Sancta on her knees, for fear of ruining her stockings. She is a careful girl, but at Falmouth the next summer she wears a bathing suit without a skirt and encourages a shy telephone lineman to take advantage after two rum cokes. The lineman gives her a multifaceted diamond, with wedding bands thrown in free. Ret gives her a kitchen shower and catches the bouquet.

In her mid-twenties, Loretta is still living at home with her parents, familiar monuments who doze on the couch after supper. They have nothing to fight about and collaborate in advice to her: "You'll end up an old maid living with a hundred cats in some tenement. You'll go queer, stuffing money under the rug, keeping your dirty underwear in greasy shopping bags. Find someone. Look, your friends have all taken the plunge."

On a singles weekend at a big hotel on Lake Placid she meets Kenny Huff. They are partnered on the treasure hunt but find nothing on their list except each other. He swallows a lot, trying to get rid of a lump in his throat that she can see moving up and down. He smells of Lifebuoy soap and Listerine. Weekends she now spends at a gravel pit, watching him fly elaborate model airplanes. He likes her to stand beside him. She expects the little planes to do more, crash or take off for more remote destinations, but they only buzz and sputter in small circles. After three windy, wet Sundays she tells him that she will have to do her laundry on Sundays.

But they are "an item." She practices writing his name after hers, thinks of them pushing a fat baby in a stroller or standing in the A&P checkout line. She can not imagine him snoring in bed beside her. They frighten each other by excessive demands. Can you make banana cream pie or grapenut pudding? Would you love me if I went bald? Will we have enough to talk about? What will happen when my teeth fall out?

She knows that he hates to travel. Their honeymoon is spent in a tropical paradise. They land at night after a delayed flight and are driven at sixty miles an hour up a winding mountain road, just missing burros and basket sellers. There has been an earthquake and the plumbing still does not work well. Precociously old girl-women brush the beach with straw brooms. Kenny has a queasy stomach that sours at lipstick on a coffee cup and sea food at the next table. He will wind up on cornflakes and soft boiled eggs. He lies in the room memorizing the schedule of return flights and executing roaches. As soon as he nods off, she tiptoes to the balcony to listen to the marimba band and to smell the tacos.

Soon there are two children. She expects their real mother to enter the house, or, more frightening, for them to slide off the road some night as Ken is driving them to pick her up at some terminus and for their car to explode in flames, tumbling down an incline, no one surviving, confirming her singleness. The children prefer Ken, of course. He takes them to the Dairy Queen, plays Chinese checkers with them, and holds them close while he pulls magic objects from their pockets. They are in awe of her, becoming silent when she appears. They treat her like a somewhat dangerously powerful stranger. Some of their best conversations are while they wait for buses to take her away or for her luggage to appear on the carousel. She remembers these intense times, rather than the spaces between.

She works in a city an hour away and is in a car pool. People sympathize with her over the distance she commutes, but she does not tell them that the drive is the best part of every day for her, especially the blizzards, ice, fogs, car breakdowns, traffic jams. Their last house is all Ken's. He is so serious about perc tests and fiberglass insulation that others consult him. He knows in advance where the sun will fall into each room and he selects every fireplace brick. She is as respectful as an uninvited guest soon to be found out. She tiptoes a lot and tries not to make much noise.

On her vacations she flies to Florida, where her old parents have moved. Ken stays home with the children. She nudges him toward association with other warm-blooded folk. Everywhere are untroubled women who would make better wives for such a wholesome man. Once, when they are sitting in the departure lounge at Logan, she tells him plain out, "You shouldn't have to put up with this. You deserve better." He replies, "It's all right. You're fine. I don't mind."

She travels to avoid breaking things. If she moves quickly enough, she will leave no traces, ruffle no surface, give no offense. People are nicer to you if you're not underfoot all the time. You become slightly more interesting upon reappearance. No one is noticing, but act as if someone is. If she lasts long enough and is in the right place by chance, she may bisect something important.

For all her worry, the children grow up and marry—one in the back-yard, the other in a Baptist chapel with her dreaming away, abstractly there. But Ken does, in a sense, die alone, in the VA hospital, no one can tell her of what. "General wear and tear," the chief resident keeps saying. She can be depended upon to visit often, although it is hard to concentrate on his dying. She composes an apology: "I'm sorry about being away so much. It is something that comes over me, I don't know what." He whispers back, "Don't worry, Ret. You just like to gallivant. I don't blame you. You'll be free now. Well fixed." She is, astonish-ingly. She never travels up to her resources, as a matter of principle.

In the company of other widows, she does the usual shrines: Knock, Lourdes, Fatima, the Rue Bac, Guadaloupe, Rome, LaSalette. Once the spiritual routine is over, they may concentrate on food. They are authorities on buffets, smorgasbords, and brunches. They especially like hot breads and dessert trays, and they carry caloric counters in their purses. Ret leaves their company for her own.

"Travel broadens," her mother observed, but Ret grows thinner and thinner. She also becomes more silent and more wise. She thinks she is storing experience. When she sees a painting of Saint John eating the gospel, she understands immediately. If I were a book, I could be read.

Someone needs what I know or can be persuaded to with a little effort.
I may die of accumulated wisdom. All this moving about must come to
something if strung on a wire.

If she could select one face or one room, she might make sense out
of the whole. Hard as she works to select one, it always flows into
another view or theme. Looking through her notebook, she confronts
fragments: a page of her name translated into various alphabets—
cyrillic, Greek, Arabic, Hindi, Hebrew; a group of phrases—thank
you, goodbye, you are kind, I want a single room, where is the wash-
room? I am thirsty.

She is always running into other nuts who are chasing something and
letting it drop through their fingers so they have to start all over again.
Some fancy a preoccupation with bird migrations or state capital domes
or topiary or chili. Some have no purpose at all. Once she was directed
to share a table in a vast hotel dining room in Kiev with a man who was
driving across Europe and Asia, barely reaching each night's stop to
which he had been routed, endlessly worried about strange road signs,
holding the map with trembling hands and magnifying glass, running
out of gas in towns where he wasn't expected, encountering police who
shouted. "I'm scared all the time," he confessed to Ret. "My wife
won't come with me after nearly dying on the Pan American Highway
and being attacked in Afghanistan. I have to do it on my own."

On a park bench in Canberra, an American with an ordinary-
sounding name told her he checked telephone directories everywhere in
the world to find anyone who spelled it his way. So far, no luck. He
had, as far as he could discover, no family. "Isn't that statistically
impossible?" she asked him. "Maybe. But it seems true in my case."
She left the bench.

She is especially interested in graves and burial chambers. Her people may be lying there in the bone pits and pot sherds. Next to those,
she likes the homes of the great and the nearly great.

Occasionally she is distracted by her companions on these excursions, like the woman from Kansas who always traveled with a three-
quarter life-sized inflatable dummy, dressed in her late husband's
cut-down pajamas. Ret would not have known about the dummy if they
had not been forced by a room shortage to share one night in Ankara,

and there the woman was, blowing up the dummy and explaining how she hated to sleep alone.

On a Trailways bus out of Memphis once, Ret saw boarding a tall, white-haired man wearing denim robes and a huge wooden cross and carrying a brown burlap bag. Before going to the back of the bus, he paused at her seat, bent close, and whispered clearly, "Have a good heart."

The summer she is fifty-three, she stands in the public library nervously staring at the classified in a journal. Sure no one is looking, she copies down "Lonely SWM, 56, fond cats, non-smoker, madrigal singer, seeks compatible traveler in realms of gold." She will not hold the cats or the madrigals against him, and she is not sure where the realms are, but she telephones the number from a phone booth. When they meet as agreed at the Capri Diner in Peapack, he seems fine, and they plan a trial run to Peru, four days including Machu Picchu. On the plane after drinking his lunch, he is airsick all the way to Lima. She rather enjoys playing the nurse's role in the Savoy Hotel until he comes at her with a broken bottle. On the return flight he sits in an aisle seat, pawing at the stewardess, and she sits at the window, holding the baby of the woman in the middle. Of course, she never sees him again after JFK but does wonder about the madrigals.

She watches occasional romance cynically. In one rainy November in Kashmir she sees a widow from Brooklyn fall in love with the owner of their dingy little houseboat, a sad-faced Moslem who constantly scratches himself under his heavy robe. "I know you think I'm crazy," she tells Ret. "But he's the first man who's smiled at me in eight years. I'll stay as long as my money holds out." In the cook boat they can see his young wife and several children. Someone is always picking up with someone, and it never seems to come out right. Two women begin sharing a cabin on the South Seas cruise at Pago Pago. By Hong Kong they are throwing drinks into each other's face. That came of expecting the wrong things out of travel.

By now Ret's native element has become motion. She is titillated by the extremes of the days, beginnings and ends. She loves awakening in strange bedrooms, reaching her feet to the floor, always a little cold.

Amazing how cold the early mornings are, even in deserts and the
tropics. Then, as she waits for coffee, even if it turns out badly, another
surge of confidence comes. And from late afternoon is another safe
time, swaying into a strange city from the airport amid decent people
going home from work, safe at last. She also enjoys driving late at
night, the feeble beams of the car or taxi picking up mysterious glints
of new places: a portico, an alley, an empty store with the smell of an
olive-wood fire, and goat bells tossing restlessly. Her fellow travelers
would be sitting silent and hopeful in the dark space while the driver
took them to their guaranteed beds.

At sixty she begins to favor the northern cities over Venetian va-
poretti or soft nights in Seville. She no longer takes moonlight carriage
rides with other American widows to hear flamenco in gypsy caves.
There is less to see and nothing surprising in the northern gray cities. It
is the tough, tight-fisted, proper landscape of her unknown grandparents, with strong coffee, cold lunches, sweet cheese, early dinner, and
off to the ski slope and the mountain hut. No one stares. They are too
busy reading their newspapers and buying new hiking boots. In the
summer the light hangs around all night long.

"Look up my second cousin, Berta, in Oslo," someone tells Ret.
"She has been an actress."

Berta's English is excellent. She may become the perfect friend for
Ret at last. They dine on exquisite plates in an ancient restaurant with
bitter-faced waiters in black suits. There are four kinds of cold fish and
huge boiled potatoes. The bill is astronomical, but Berta is rich.

She tells Ret, "My life is so tragic I must share it with you. We are
heart mates. You will understand. I can no longer bear the suffering.
My husband has gone blind and my beautiful, titian-haired daughter is
dying. Every day she is more frail. It will kill my good husband too.
He thinks she has a stubborn virus. Even sitting beside her holding her
thin hand he does not suspect yet. Oh, that sickroom is so oppressive.
The lace curtains blow in and out. The breeze is so fresh and hopeful.
My thin, wonderful daughter stretches out her hands toward the garden
sweetness." Berta begins to cry. Grape-sized tears form and drop on the
starched tablecloth. Then her shoulders shake. The tablecloth is becoming very damp.

Ret insists upon accompanying Berta home, where her neat husband has just driven in from the laboratory and his only child, a son, is walking the golden retriever. "Poor Berta," the husband whispers to Ret, "thinks she is in a life painted by Edvard Munch. We will have to send her away for a rest again. It is better you should leave now."

Ret has become a proficient over-listener. "It is only because I have had such practice being alone," she says, self-deprecatingly. "If there were anyone to listen, I would talk to them and make them talk back. But better second hand than none."

In Stockholm she hears a British couple planning a mass execution and then discovers that they are discussing rats in their basement at home, but the American mother-in-law in Helsinki really hates her son's new bride. The day that the girl finally throws her room key at the old lady's head and stalks out of the dining room, no one misses a mouthful. The waiter picks up the key. The son thanks his mother, "I never liked her anyway."

The better to hear bits and pieces of narrative, she hides in parks and plazas behind a camera. Despite blurs and misjudgments, enough curious views survive for her to be asked to entertain shut-ins with them. The recreation director advances threateningly, all teeth, "And where are you going to take us today?" Her memories are as fragmented as slides, illuminated by anecdotes like firefly glow.

She wonders how she looks in snapshots or slides other tourists may have taken. "Who's that little gray woman beside the balloon seller? Do you remember her name? No. Funny lady. Now wait till you see this next slide of the belly dancer." Actually, she wears brown and rust more than gray. She scorns the washing routines that use up time, but she does have her hair done everywhere. Not for her hair, but for the companionship, the cheery voices, the satisfied final look in the mirror, another sign that the world is still running. As dependable as bread, the connective tissue across continents. She buys bread everywhere.

There are times when none of this wandering makes any sense. She walks through foreign weather in her tidy coat, being shouted at in languages she will never learn. She is as skinny as driftwood. However, her only visible maladies are a slightly stiff heart and brain.

She travels in the suburbs of violence. The wrecks, crashes, and bombs are always for others. In Argentina she is led from the hotel before the explosion. A month after her visit, she watches on Japanese television the holocaust of a department store in Brussels. A plate-glass window falls from the fourth floor of a Reno casino to kill a woman from Edmonton, while Ret turns the corner. She is getting ready for the violence marked for her. It never comes. Her suitcase is never lost. Her stomach never rebels.

Briefly home in her house, or really Kenny Huff's house, so unfamiliar is she with its spaces that she misses one of the back steps and falls the rest of the way onto the flagstone, shattering her hip.

So she does wind up at home in Vera's Senior Retreat. Every morning as she hears the heat rise and the night shift of nurses depart, she begins to struggle with her restraints. "Stop that," they say to her as she tries to brush aside the spoons of breakfast cereal. In her head is the perfect getaway scheme. She will get to the hall pay phone, call a taxi, be let off at the Greyhound terminal, and get on anything leaving. The left side of her body does not work any more.

"Tell her she's been there. Maybe she'll believe it, and that'll shut her up," the charge nurse tells the aide.

The aide explains patiently, "You must be very tired. You have been on a long trip. Now you've come home."

Light Timber*

My Uncle Jude was a throwback, everybody agreed. He would have
liked to have been in the mainstream but lost his way. Jude was my
mother's brother, only son in the family, which, I suppose, was part of
his problem. My using his first name, by the way, shows no disrespect.
He was fond of saying that he was a simple sort, which in some ways
was true. He disliked the rain and the calls of doves or pigeons, but he
was something of a crepe hanger and liked to read the obituaries and
visit the old in nursing homes, and he always teared up when he heard
"O Promise Me" or "Some Sweet Day."

He was my godfather, and until I was about ten, he was my favorite
person. His pockets held gifts to be searched for: tin whistles, measur-
ing tape, yo-yos, barrettes, thimbles, once even a compass. For me he
furnished a whole doll's house piece by piece and before that a tiny
farm with wooden animals and barns and fuzzy hedges and little
fences. But by the time I got into junior high, he'd faded considerably
from my life. Oh, he took all of us—mother and dad and the aunts and
married uncles, cousins, and my closest friend—to dinner at the Show
Boat restaurant after my confirmation and always remembered my
birthday with crisp bills, even when I was working after college in New
York. He probably made a list of anniversaries and birthdates and had
the bills all ready for sending with a carefully addressed card.

Of course, the mail was an important part of his life. After the Army,
he became a mail carrier, and when his legs gave out he was promoted

*Sawmill operators originally used this term to differentiate pine from oak, etc. The
word came to mean superficial, shallow.

to sorting in the main post office. Something had happened to his feet—
frostbite, probably, during the war. For a long time after the war, my
mother kept all the letters and cards he had sent her, although they said
almost nothing. "Paris is like any other big town. Can't find anything
like home cooking. Six months more before I see God's country. Yours
in haste." Then she must have thrown them out. I was searching yesterday for a scrap of his handwriting but couldn't find any. Because as an
adult I always found conversation in person or on paper with him
awkward, I flinched guiltily when I saw again his black scrawls on the
birthday cards and heard his voice sometimes during Thanksgiving or
Christmas telephone calls. As with those we hear only in chorus, it is
hard to recall his voice, and we made no tapes and took few pictures in
my family. Those pictures in which he can be seen show only his head
in the back row behind his sisters and their families. His shyness turned
to frown.

On the job, he stooped on account of his bad feet and, perhaps, as a
result of growing up in a house full of small women. Like most mail
carriers, he was full of cheery patter. "Oh, don't call me Mr. McNa-
marra. Jude's the name. Not Judas. Jude. For the patron saint of lost
causes. My mother must have thought I needed all the help I could get.
A hardship case. Well, take it nice and easy."

Another reason Jude walked unevenly was that he was always looking
up, not at the sky, but at trees. Nobody in our family was interested in
gardening, except to keep grass in its place. And in Jude's generation
they were still congratulating themselves on having escaped being
farmers in County Clare. Jude went over on an Aer Lingus flight from
Boston to Shannon to help the cousins hay one July. "We're well out of
all that," he used to tell me.

It was trees that he cared about. "I don't know why. They try so
hard. They give a lot and don't ask much. All that ice and smog and
cutting back from the wires. And all the different shapes they grow
into. You never know. It's all inside, telling them, but not letting us
know until it comes out." In passing, he sometimes touched the trunks
of the trees along his route—the last of the sickly elms, some old
maples, ailanthus coming sturdily along through cracks in the pavement. First, he set out a couple of dwarf fruit trees in back of my
grandmother's three decker. "They give a good harvest with little

space." Then he put in a row of poplars, over my father's protest that they would be dead in thirty years. "Time enough for me," Jude answered. Whenever we saw him reading, it seemed to be about trees, their leaves and bark and root systems. The few times in recent years that I was in that gloomy parlor for grandmother's birthday parties, Jude would be going out onto the back porch to stare at the branches of his fruit trees. He would make detours on the way to the garage or incinerator to look some more.

When I was growing up, the family would have described themselves as close. They saw each other on Sundays and in between called on the phone. They all lived within about a twenty-five-mile radius, and when they said The Family we all knew what they meant. They didn't go in for elaborate explanations but instead seemed to operate by subtle signaling like flocks of birds. They shared a prejudice against extreme behavior; my mother distrusted patriotic or religious displays. You didn't have to hang a dozen family photographs to show that you cared about the subjects. Excesses of religious piety like Holy Thursday altars at home or Fatima statues in the front yard were simply embarrassing. My parents generally regretted the noisy social confusion resulting from the English Mass—the handshakes, the unmelodic hymns, all the odd moving around. They missed the dreamy quiet of the Latin Mass, although neither of them knew Latin.

Like Jude's devotion to trees, his religious enthusiasm was a respected mystery to us. We assumed that it took the place of wife and children for him. At forty-five, after Vatican II, he seemed to have come into his own. He was elected to the newly formed Parish Council. He passed the basket at an early Sunday mass and, finally, he became a lector. He used to practice the reading up in his room so that he wouldn't stumble over the difficult place names in the Epistles. "Your uncle," my father muttered, glancing toward the ceiling from which Jude's unmodulated voice was solemnly describing Paul's travels, "Your uncle should have been born a church mouse."

It was about this time that he began to notice Sister Stanislas Kostka, who was often on reception duty at St. Jerome's convent. Probably, the first time, he rang the bell with a special delivery letter and, falling apart in her immediate presence, he rattled on about the wet spring good for saplings, mold, and the infield grass at Fenway. It was always safe to talk with nuns about baseball. This was before the modifications began, and she was in the old habit, an impressive eighteenth-century widow's costume.

It was also considered, in those days, that it was all right to joke a lot but gently with the sisters and even, outside of the classroom, to call them by familiar nicknames. Of course, she was Sister Stash. She had come from a Polish family in another part of the state and was their first religious in generations. Once they got over that shock, they canonized her, driving up to the convent on Sundays in their big red Buicks to cart her off with another sister for an expensive dinner in some fancy relish-tray restaurant. They would dance around her, laughing and smiling. She was their talisman. New babies were brought to sit on her lap; her nephews made her elaborately tooled missal covers at camp; her father provided styrofoam hampers of kielbasa; and her brother told her frequently how lucky she really was.

At the end of one summer, I came home from waitressing on the Cape to get ready for my last year at college. It was Labor Day, when the huge parish fair is always held. It grows bigger every year. They raffle off a new Mercury, which is the central attraction; import through a concessionaire several fairly dull rides on which no one can get hurt; offer free blood-pressure tests; provide a different band every night; and serve two sittings of a cheap shore dinner of chowder, clam cakes, and watermelon. And, of course, there are the tables of fancy work and white elephants. Jude led me toward the jewelry table behind which Sister Stash was installed. That year the jewelry was especially ugly; the table featured bead necklaces, name bracelets, little animals painted on shells, ceramic pansies. Sister Stash was sitting on a folding chair behind the table, looking out in a dazed, indifferent way. She was in the newly modified habit, which added ten years and several pounds to any wearer. It included a mid-calf skirt, high-necked blouse, and a little cotton head scarf.

I wasn't surprised that Jude stopped at the table. He was a compulsive buyer of books of chances and lottery tickets. "Never know when our ship will come in." He was a pushover for any Sunday solicitors for causes or kids unloading giant candy bars for Little League or holding canisters for band uniforms.

"I want you to pick out some earrings," he said, "anything you want." He seemed quite nervous. "This is my niece Molly, Sister

Stash. I want her to have something nice. Remember, I told you she's the one up at State. She could be a lawyer some day."

I was surprised that he had mentioned me to her at all. We stood uncomfortably in front of the card table looking at shells awkwardly glued to earrings and sea horses stuck in plastic. I couldn't see a possibility in the whole lot. Looking across into Sister Stash's eyes, I thought she recognized my dilemma, but her expression never revealed. Her face was like a doll's, perfect without being memorable or beautiful. Because her lips were often parted, she looked about to say something. The white blouse and kerchief gave her the look of a sturdy peasant.

Jude must have had a beer or two at the rathskeller tent (they were featuring a German theme at the fair that year). He had a low tolerance for drinking; it made him silly and sleepy. He held up a pair of tiered, sparkling earrings to his own ear lobes, against his large, flushed face.

Sister Stash looked confused and was rather abrupt: "You'll take those?"

"What a saleswoman you make," he said. "Come on, Molly, don't you want to buy some Christmas gifts for your chums?"

I asked Sister Stash what grade she would be teaching next year, and she said, "Who knows? They never tell you until the day school opens. I guess it doesn't matter."

"They'll be lucky kids, whichever ones they are," Jude said. And as we walked away, he was still holding the earrings, which he fortunately forgot to give me. "What a wonderful spirit that woman has," he said.

A few weeks before the Christmas after that fair, I had a strange telephone call from my mother. She always waited for cheaper rates, and she never called in the morning. When I heard her strained voice, I thought that grandmother had gone.

"No, it's worse than that, if you can imagine."

"What?" I asked, shivering in the ugly dorm phone booth, trying to keep my voice calm.

"It's Jude. He wants to get married. To Sister Stash. That is, Rose— whatever her real name is."

"Maybe he's in love," I said.

"How could he be? Jude? Why, he hardly knows her. She's coming out, though."

"Well, that's lucky. They couldn't very well live in the convent," I said.

"Don't be smart," she said. "There's nothing funny about this. I wanted you to know so that you can plan to go somewhere else for Christmas if you want. It's going to be terrible around here. The embarrassment. The bad luck. What did we ever do to deserve this?"

"I don't see that he's done anything wrong," I said. "He's a good man. A lot better than most."

"That's just it. Your father says it's like a cow that gives a fine pail of milk and then kicks it over."

It was impossible to discover where my father got these comparisons. "Where is Jude now?" I asked. "Shouldn't I congratulate him?"

"He's upstairs fixing his breakfast," my mother replied.

"Well, he won't have to do that any more," I said.

My mother ignored that comment. Jude's making his own breakfast had always seemed the ultimate loneliness. He was meticulous about the details, setting out the coffee cup and plate the night before with the knife and spoon and one paper napkin.

About the wedding, we were torn between confusion and curiosity. By now I was so absorbed in college life that what I was seeing at home was distanced as if in some fairly dull and coarse-grained film.

So many religious were then leaving the orders that Sister Stash's request for release from vows was processed rapidly, and the simple one-page document arrived back from Rome in no time at all. Rose (we had to remember to call her that) was waiting at the Motherhouse to be fetched. On the first day of my Christmas vacation, my mother and I, somewhat like chaperons, drove up there with Jude. I didn't see them greet each other. He rang the door bell and went inside, returning quickly with her and a small suitcase. She may have gone shopping earlier or perhaps they gave her a navy-blue polo coat which was too long and a few sizes too big. We had the car radio on and sang along with the Christmas carols, then stopped at a Friendly's. Rose pushed the BLT around her plate, while Jude ate heartily.

She stayed in my parents' apartment since her family was still so scandalized by her coming out that no one among them could be mustered to communicate, let alone participate in the ceremony. Therefore, there was no point in delaying the wedding, and the holidays ran together in confusion. Jude was a changed man, laughing, touching things, waving his hands in the air, but I never saw him embrace her.

Rose and I went shopping once before the wedding. Used to the company of women, she talked more with me than in the house with Jude. She went busily through the crowded shopping mall, feeling fabrics, picking over the bargain tables, and finally selected a markeddown, street-length, blue wool dress that she could wear later. Although the order had become much less strict, she had ten years to make up for. I wasn't used to seeing her in bright colors, and she tended to buy everything a size too big. Since they were taking a package tour to Acapulco, she also bought a bathing suit. The whole idea of their honeymoon seemed indiscreet to me.

We tried to make the wedding as festive as we could, but it was clear that we were all on edge, bumping into each other and talking too loudly. They were married at a ten o'clock mass on the day after Christmas. Our timing was way off. The ceremony was very brief, and we got to the Mona Lisa Lounge too early. They hadn't set up the tables for lunch, and even the bar wasn't open. Rose observed that this wedding had been a good deal shorter than the other one. That was the only funny thing anyone said.

After the drinks and food arrived, matters improved. Then, as so often, my father surprised me. He had stood up for Jude, and as best man was expected to offer the toast. He must have searched through the biblical glossary for the one he gave. He made some reference to Jude as a tree planter and then he quoted Isaiah, "As the days of a tree are the days of my people, and the works of their hands shall be of long continuance." My father has a lovely voice and he spoke with real conviction, as if making up for years of slighting Jude. The tension broke for a while, and we noisily got into our cars and congregated on the observation deck of our shabby little state airport to see them off. Rose was wearing her polo coat, to which she had pinned the orchid corsage. She seemed not to walk with Jude as much as to run ahead with a bunch of strangers. He stood behind, waving repeatedly to us.

Then we drove back home, uneasy and not wanting to separate. My father said over the old fashioned that it was the oddest Christmas he ever wanted to spend.

Family gatherings after that time maintained the tension. It took some getting used to thinking of Jude as married, and he was busy creating a cult for her. She was often absent, in her sewing room or shopping, when he talked about her. When she did appear, she was as elusive as a breeze. She looked different from the rest of us. We are swarthy Irish like big shade trees. She was light and supple as a birch, the leaves glistening like ghosts. Jude was totally absorbed by her, plying her continually with questions. Should he wear the black necktie with the green suit? Should they cash in the matured savings bonds? Should they take up line dancing? Could she explain existentialism simply to him? All the while she seemed to be looking sideways to escape his scrutiny. Or perhaps she was dreaming with her eyes open. Her answers were minimal.

Once he said to me, "She's so quiet she scares me. I don't know what's going on in her mind. Remembering, I suppose. She's been through so much."

And sometimes when we were all sitting around after dinner, he would try to lead her into the conversation. "Hey, Rose, tell them about almost setting the novitiate on fire when you were scrambling eggs after lights out." She would protest, "It wasn't that funny. They wouldn't be interested." And quite lamely she would begin the story. We felt compelled to laugh far more than it deserved, which may have convinced Jude that she was witty. But anyone looking carefully at her impassive face and twisting hands knew otherwise. Occasionally she would interrupt the stories with a sigh as if the weight of the words troubled her tongue, and Jude would finish them.

They had been married two years when she left him, apparently not for anyone else. Simply for herself. Not that we ever really got the whole story. Maybe there was no one episode, probably no great disagreement, and there was no divorce. So quiet were they that the rest of the family did not discover the loss until she had been gone a few days. It was certainly inconceivable that they would have shouted or cried out or thrown things at each other or slammed doors. She may have figured out finally that he had married her for what she represented or what he thought she represented.

To everyone but Jude her departure caused little dislocation. They had continued to live in the top-floor apartment of my grandmother's three decker. So there Jude stayed, among all his things, having, one might say, the run of the house, looking in on the other relatives and out at his trees.

"You were right to plant those poplars. They'll be here long after us. That's for sure," my father repeatedly told him.

My cousins and I were busy with our lives, falling in and out of love, marrying and unmarrying, preferring to believe that all of our old life was waiting for us, back there, capable of being taken up, though we seldom tested it.

Jude's was the first death in the family. He was rushed to the hospital by his buddies when he slumped over the postal sorting desk one afternoon and then suffered two massive coronaries, almost too grand an ailment for his modesty.

Until then, our family had escaped death and, summoned with no preparation, we all stood around Grady's Funeral Home in unfamiliar dark clothes, wrong for the season. It was July and humid. While gardens were heavy with zinnias and marigolds, mid-July is not a good season in New England for floral sprays.

Over the whir of the air conditioner, we tried to cheer each other up, to get used to the circumstance. We had not realized that our ceremonies had always been happy—weddings, christenings, graduations. I suppose Jude had attended a lot of wakes and funerals. He would have been in his element. What strikes me often is how reduced so much of modern ritual is. For instance, wakes aren't what they used to be, or parades or family picnics or Sunday dinner. Maybe they never were what they were supposed to be. Even summers aren't as good any more.

Naturally, we were all thinking about Rose, who now lives on the West Coast under mysterious circumstances in something like a commune. There was a pay phone in that place and all sorts of background noises—children, shouts, and barking dogs—according to my cousin who was given the responsibility of informing her of Jude's death without encouraging her to attend the funeral. There had been no danger of that. She expressed sympathy to everyone, thanked him for calling, and said goodbye.

"Can you imagine," my mother said, "she didn't even send a flower. Ashamed, I suppose."

"Light timber," my father said in an uncontrolled voice. He was more shaken than any of us, perhaps because he was closer to Jude in age. I had never seen him cry before, and great untidy tears rained over his face. "That girl was light timber."

Pen Pals

Claire's mother put a high value on loyalty, especially to friends. New ones were silver; old ones, gold. Her mother treasured several golden oldies, wrote back and forth to a dozen such wonders: Dearest Kitten, Sweet Sue, Dear Maudie, Love & Kisses to the Bunch of You. Tell Hubby Hello, Remember the Good Old Days, Here's a picture of Claire on her tricycle. Her mother turned her life inside out for the world to see, without stitches as she remade it. She lived by clichés. Everything came out finally for the best.

Claire was not a great one for having close friends. For a while a thin-faced state child named Hilda had attached herself, trying to exchange lunch boxes and barrettes. Claire sent her on unpleasant errands and stared at her freckles. "You don't have to be so mean. You go out of your way," Hilda said. And finally, not meaning it, "I hate you," which was a relief for Claire. Anyway, she was happiest when counting and wrapping pennies and checking the latest entry in her school passbook account.

It was hard to see the potential for long friendships in the third grade. When they studied geography, Sister Charles-Marie produced a worldwide list from a mission magazine: French girl, aged fourteen, collects Sinatra records and cowboy singer autographs, keen on sports; Canadian boy, aged twelve, polio shut-in, will exchange matchbooks and train schedules. From that list Claire got her pen pal, Rose: English girl, aged ten, likes horses and singing.

Such relationships are supposed to last for three intense months and then tire out because of summer vacation or waiting too long for replies or running out of news. This one lasted forever, or almost, at least for Rose's ever and next to that for Claire.

At first the letters were full of essential information. Rose lived in Liverpool. Her parents, originally from Limerick but coming up in the world, had sent her to a Sacred Heart boarding school in the country. She wrote Claire during her recreation hour on Saturday afternoons, after embroidery and ironing and French conversation. She revealed that she was good at sums, liked caramels, had chicken pox scars, had lost five best friends there at school, and had written a boy in Australia who had not replied.

Claire tried to explain her home town, Waterbury, to Rose. After several crossouts, she wrote, "This is a fairly old and far-away city. We drive to Watertown on Sunday afternoons and buy Good Humors. Toasted Almond is my favorite. I will go to Radio City for the Easter show. Could you send me lots of coins?"

"She will not know where Watertown is. What do you mean by far-away city?" Claire's father asked, reading over her shoulder.

"She will not understand Toasted Almond," her mother pointed out.

Then they lost interest. The letters were already very tiring to read and to answer. Rose wrote faithfully every Saturday. In the first year she sent two souvenirs—a transparent bracelet made from a shaving of the windscreen of a Spitfire bomber and a salt-and-pepper set, the salt with George VI and the pepper with Elizabeth, both smiling. Claire sent a jigsaw puzzle of the USA, every state a different color. Rose sent a snapshot from her summer holiday at Brighton. As advertised, she was small, with unfortunately bucked teeth but nice hair. Between two well-wrapped giants, her parents, she squinted toward the murky sea.

After the summer all the other pen pals had become strangers. Claire regretted missing that opportunity. Perhaps Rose did too. Pity the poor wartime censors having to go through discussions of school dances, poison ivy, cable stitches, whiteheads, friendship bracelets, crushes. Will it never end, Claire wondered.

"You are like me, an old-fashioned girl," Claire's mother said. "You are even more loyal than I. But you have to be. I made you." Her mother collected rose petals, dried them, and stuffed them into old stockings. They rustled in the bureau drawers. She knew only the first lines of songs, which she sang over and over as she dusted. She repeated useful rules for growing girls: "Don't answer the telephone on the first ring; Look happy; Make your eyes work for you; Play your cards wisely; Remember, your mother is your best friend."

What Claire loved was Flash Gordon, Wonder Woman, War Bonds, anything up-to-date. She wanted to slam the door on memory and take up the first berth on a rocket ship. Given her grandmother's garnet necklace, she deliberately broke the delicate clasp. She favored pop-it pearls and rhinestones. She yearned to make first-string cheerleader but, failing to jump high enough, she settled for a Saturday job in Liggett's and saved $2,000.

Rose dropped French and embroidery in favor of shorthand and typing, and the horses were carted away from her school, probably to be eaten, she feared. "You haven't replied for two months," she wrote. "Did I say something to offend you?" At Christmas she sent a lumpy tea cloth.

"Such nice linen," Claire's mother observed. "It's too bad that she used such cheap thread." It had blotted into red circles.

Playing her advantage, Claire sent nylons. "I have a boyfriend," she reported. "He is twenty-one and in the Navy Air Force. His name is Bob and he gave me a solid silver bracelet."

Bob flew away. Claire went to college, saw her first cockroach, met a Communist, smoked a reefer, thought she was in love with her section man in Western Civ. but didn't make out, only fumbled around on his cot in the proctor's quarters. None of this was suitable for discussion with Rose, who had joined an insurance group and talked passionately about holiday tours to Scotland, Paris, and Fatima. She sent dishtowels and spoons from everywhere and had perfect memory of every meal in the favorite hotels in which she installed her parents for holidays in New Forest or along the Wye or in the Valley of the Boyne. From the photographs, it was obvious that Rose was growing into an only slightly younger version of her mother. She favored dark print dresses—black or navy-blue splashed with roses and violets and columbine, topped with puff sleeves and crocheted lace collars fixed by white-gold bar pins with sapphires and moonstones in filagreed nests. Her handwriting was square and labored; the spelling, erratic. For a while she tried to introduce her associates at work, six women of almost identical circumstances—Ivy, Lily, Cecily, Hilary, Elsie, and Minnie. Considering them putting out their tea mugs and talking about Rose's American friend depressed Claire.

"Goodbye," Claire kept suggesting. "Thanks for the model of the Eiffel Tower and the bank in the shape of St. Paul's, but Goodbye." The weekend before graduation she spent with her latest boyfriend at his parents' cottage in Manchester-by-the-Sea. It was late May, and he was supposedly opening the cottage. After taking off the storm windows, he proposed. His father was the superintendent of a mental hospital, but he seemed unmarked by the experience of growing up with crazies for playmates. Within the proposal, he mentioned the fringe benefits of his new job. Claire had overestimated his prospects.

Meanwhile, Rose not only had aging parents and her flute but, after a novena to St. Jude, a boyfriend named Gordon. He worked in a butcher shop, but the problem was that he was Methodist. They would try to work that out. He too had old parents.

Claire moved to New York, worked in a bank, took up tennis, got engaged to a partner in mixed doubles, completed her silver flatware pattern, married. She and her husband, an energetic lawyer, looked even better in their photographs than in real life.

When she moved into selling expensive real estate, photographs of her smiling beside the flowers or staring into the glowing fireplace decorated the fancy brochures of the realtor who quickly made her a partner. "You have a killer instinct for property," he reflected when she bought him out. By 1970 her husband told her that he had discovered himself finally and wanted a divorce so that he could go off with his secretary to Seattle and become a fisherman. Claire was not surprised. It was an excellent time to turn his generous property settlement into apartment houses that could be converted into classy condominiums.

All this action provided narrative, slightly edited, for writing to Rose. Their letters now ran in safe patterns featuring little successes, fun vacations, and extreme weather. Bad news was avoided. Rose sanitized her parents' decay into an extended Victorian episode. Gordon had disappeared entirely.

One might ask why they had not met in such a small world. Claire had to make a deliberate effort to avoid England entirely on her first European trips. She had actually flown in and out of London several times and was in the last of a three-week stay when she announced herself to Rose in a trunk call. They met the next day in Paddington Station at the W. Smith kiosk.

"So here you are," Claire said, wanting to flee. "After all this time." She held her hand out stiffly to prevent Rose's embrace.

At the end of the day, Rose did cling a little before getting on the return train, wiping away tears. "I always wanted a sister, but you're even better." Before that was a sort of lunch in the cafeteria at the Victoria and Albert. It was raining, and there was always something to look at there. Rose would have preferred lace but could be persuaded to stare at coins and snuffboxes. She chewed her food carefully and thought a long time before announcing, "We could be twins. We have so much in common."

What they had in common Claire could have listed on the smallest file card with space left over—blue eyes, birthdays two months apart, one grandmother apiece named Sheila, and a death grip on what they valued. For Rose that was their friendship and what she described as "my little home," as if it were a third person to whom Claire had to be introduced. "Next time we have to meet in my little home," she insisted. Claire imagined a rubber tree and an aspidistra, dark rooms, a moldy vestibule, the mixed smells of talcum powder and floor wax, and the sort of meals that women cook for themselves, like cheese omelets and tuna fish casserole. There would be calendars with cute cats and pin cushions in tomato shapes.

"Perhaps next year," Claire promised on each Christmas card. But they did not meet again. Rose talked a great deal about her pension and finally retired. She was grateful for cards from Akron, Salt Lake, Little Rock, and Vegas. Claire traveled so much closing deals and looking at prospects that she could often not remember the name of the city as she slid her feet toward the motel's shag rug.

On her birthday card (they were forty-seven), Rose had apologized, "I'll send your gift as soon as I leave the hospital. I miss my home but it's a little change being surrounded by people. They're doing some tests. I haven't been myself recently."

Claire imagined Rose scuttling around the busy hospital, smiling and wincing, glad for the company. She wired flowers at an absurd cost. Rose's birthday gift to her arrived, a tufted plaid sateen tea cozy with another message, "I'm resting here for a while after the surgery. Such a pretty day. There is a nice view from my room of a playground. All day children's voices come through the window. One of the ladies who is kind to me is writing this letter until my arm is strong enough."

The day that the letter came from Rose's solicitor, Claire's firm was in the last stage of selling a renovated mill complex in Bridgeport. The client took a rollover mortgage, and someone produced a bottle of champagne. At the afternoon's end, there was a cluster of styrofoam cups holding stubbed-out cigarettes on her desk. There on top of the opened mail was the solicitor's letter. Rose had died ten days before, after a brave struggle, he was sorry to report. Claire had inherited her house. It was assumed that she would complete the necessary papers and assume ownership promptly.

Of course, she put off the trip as long as possible. Months later, after her flight to London and the long train ride into the Midlands and a melancholy interview in the law chambers, the solicitor gave her directions to Rose's house and called a cab. He was elderly and wore an ancient suit and dense glasses through which he peered at Claire. Holding the door of the taxi, he said, "You must understand, she thought the world of you. No one dearer or closer."

"We were old friends," Claire admitted, "of an unusual sort."

"True friends are beyond price," he said.

Rose's house was not as bad as she had expected. "You'll have to get at that garden," the driver said, not understanding the circumstances. He was referring to the rusty snapdragons and the top-heavy cosmos in the front yard.

The neighbor from next door struggled with the double lock. "It's so sad. Her home was her whole world. Like a monument. But I guess you know all about her, being so close for so long. You'll want to be alone now, I fancy."

Once she walked into the hallway, Claire knew what every drawer and closet would contain. There would be balls of neatly wound string and flattened paper from packages, stacks of emery boards, lace collars laid out in old tissue paper, neatly darned stockings in balls. On the dining room table a silver pheasant bent, searching for something on the lace cloth. On the dressing table blocking the bedroom window was a darkened ivory hairbrush with Rose's initials.

In the kitchen the blue willow dishes were ranked by size, and the hobnailed glasses were carefully turned over on a towel. "I could make myself tea," Claire thought, "but then I might never leave."

On the walls she expected and found Millet's *Gleaners* beside the Angelus, opposite Burne-Jones's *King Cophetua and the Beggar Maid* and in the parlor *Sir Galahad* in a fancy frame. Upstairs her own photograph smiled from one wall toward another of the *Pietà,* against such a black background that it looked like soap sculpture.

She pulled open the drawers of Rose's bureau. They slid easily. Inside, resting lightly on the scented paper, were slips and nightgowns too good to wear. The bottom drawer was unusually heavy. Of course, it was full of her letters, arranged by years, tied carefully. Thirty-five years of letters. She closed the drawer.

She had a gift for estimating the value of property, an enviable gift. She was already thinking that if she tore out a wall or two, painted over the oak, fixed up the back garden, the house would bring a good price.

Safe Home

Whatever she did, Becky Pearce wore goodness. No matter how old she got to be, she remained the perennial good girl. At least she knew better.

She was a weaver. The town knew vaguely that she was famous elsewhere for her craft. A glossy travel magazine had featured her house, making it look larger, tidier than it really was. Strangers drove tentatively through the town and asked directions to her place.

But to the town she remained the daughter of the painter who had become famous for his clouds and skies. Becky had gone on living in his studio, a rambling, weathered series of huge rooms, shrouded by wisteria, a summer place originally. There was a della Robbia in a niche in the garden wall, and three copper beech trees were taking over the lawn. "Oh, it was my parents who were the interesting ones," Becky protested. "I'm only a spider. They were like butterflies."

That was the way she faded, the perfect daughter of the painter. No matter that she had once been a wife and mother herself, and had failed at both. Past danger, she was a solitary success. She had clinched her reputation as honorable and lucky, incapable of malice. Like most legends, it was partially true. She recycled her trash, baked good bread, kept a compost heap, converted to wood stoves, and wore a slight smile. In the pretty town everyone spoke well of her—the piano tuner, the Agway couple, the superintendent of the dump, the librarian, the plumber. She was past worrying or thinking much about.

Long ago, during the war, Becky had married the first man who had asked her because she sensed that there might be no other. They met at a USO Buddies Club dance and marrying him had seemed vaguely patriotic. He had seemed funny, a trait quite missing in her life. He was a hugger, and in her spacious, high-minded household there hadn't been much hugging. His letters were soon full of repeated erotic promises which excited her greatly. She couldn't use the words back to him, but she played them over in her mind until the hairs on her forearms rose.

When she brought him home on his first leave, her parents were unimpressed. "Are you sure he's right for you? Shouldn't you meet his people? Don't be hasty. Shouldn't you think about it a little longer?" They were great thinkers about their lives.

When she finally went south with her new husband to visit his home town, it was already obvious that she had made the first mistake: she was carrying his child. There were more discoveries, none pleasing. His father ran a used-car lot, and his mother worked in a luncheonette. They had given up being cheerful and lived in a dark bungalow in an old mining town where slag heaps and repeated floods competed to discourage trees and grass. His father had a beer can collection in the den, and his mother made dolls out of Pepsi bottles, with crocheted clothes and cute cardboard faces.

Becky tried to pry her way into their lives but gave up when she couldn't find the openings. The fatback and greens exaggerated her morning sickness. When her new father-in-law twitted her about having one in the oven, just making it under the nine months' wire, she didn't know whether to smile or pretend she hadn't heard.

"Now that he doesn't get enough in this house, he can't keep his mind off it," her mother-in-law said. One of her incisors was black.

Although there were little plaster-cast nudes in the painter's studio and Becky's mother had patiently explained, with the right names, the intricacies of intercourse to her even before she was curious, her parents had seemed to regret sex, as if it were unfortunate that such sweaty awkwardness had to accompany love. They read aloud to each other in the gazebo after dinner in the summer, and her father was always clipping the most exquisite rose as payment for breakfast.

Her mother-in-law wanted to know if artists shared wives, had she posed naked for her dad, didn't she want a little nooky right now instead of sitting in the den with the beer cans. It was a short visit.

Becky and her husband drove south across the border and rented a house on Lake Chapala.

"We might as well enjoy ourselves while we can," he said. But he had already lost interest in going to bed in the afternoon.

As far as she could tell, he had been faithful to her for six months until one afternoon when she returned sooner than expected from the market. Not finding him in the courtyard, she saw that their bedroom door was ajar, and she pressed it open silently. Lunging over the round body of the girl-woman who came with the house was his bare back. She had just begun to be able to look at that back in the mornings as he was dressing.

There were tears and a standoff. He spent the afternoons at Juan's Nueva York Café. Shortly after their child, Jo, was born in the Mexican American Hospital in Guadalajara, he disappeared entirely, along with the station wagon and the contents of the checking account.

Becky flew home, of course. Her parents and their town had been on her side all along, but they never reminded her of it. They expunged the marriage and husband entirely from memory. After all, it was a long-completed town, whose only mysteries were occasional arrowheads turned up each spring by gardeners extending their borders. Within thirty miles in every direction were enough people with whom to play Scrabble, walk through the rhododendrons, car pool to the symphony, and rake cranberries.

At first, Becky selected the role of Insecure Retainer; then she assumed Ageless Good Girl. Until they became frail and dependent, her parents traveled a lot, leaving her to keep their house and tend the troublesome, strange child. As a baby Jo was a ruthless crier, most angrily when she awakened and during the whole day for reasons Becky could not figure. The pediatrician plotted strategies: how to hold Jo, when not to respond, what the cries might signify, whether she was allergic to dogs, grass, horses, people. Becky marked the days by the number of aspirin and whether Jo was as bad or worse than the day before. As soon as she could walk, she tried running away.

The first psychologist suggested intense empathy, sitting on the floor with Jo and looking out through her eyes at the world, trying to phrase her complaints: "You want to run away forever," "You feel unhappy about having to eat these eggs," "It hurts to have your hair combed,"

"You're tearing the stuffing out of the bear to show Mommie how you hate taking a bath." Becky thought she played this game well, but her talent was lost on Jo.

The next stage was total permissiveness: Jo bolted into her own room, picking ravioli with her fingers from the jar and throwing it at the walls, once squeezing and drinking pokeberry juice and then having her stomach pumped out. In the third grade she pushed the class terrarium out the window and cut the heads off six baby hamsters before the teacher was able to restrain her.

The psychiatrist whom they saw together and separately predicted that thirteen would be a crucial year. It was. Jo was locked into her room for days of silence. Becky lay on a mattress on the floor outside, muttering pleas and promises under the door in a low voice, ashamed that her parents might hear. They probably did, since they left suddenly on a birding trip to the southwest.

By the end of that summer her father had completed his last important series of sky paintings, Clouds Now and Then, inspired by Basho. The day he had hung the twelve to show the total effect to Becky before shipping them to his gallery, Jo set the fire. Fortunately she ran out of kerosene, and the volunteer fire department was efficient. Only one of the skies needed restoration, but the studio roof had to be replaced. "Don't fret," her father told Becky, "it was time to reshingle, anyway."

It was no use pretending that it hadn't happened. Becky had taken up meditation to reduce tension and anxiety. She asked Jo to sit silently with her for fifteen minutes after meals, at the end of which Jo fled the house, slamming every door on her way to the bowling alley, which was the center of her social life. Becky could see her slamming doors of strange cars down at the entrance to their drive, but Jo never brought any of the occupants beyond the mail box, although there were cokes and snacks waiting in the fridge. Sitting in the darkness at midnight and watching the road, Becky waited for the headlights to stop and drop their passenger.

The new psychiatrist suggested a broader margin between them. He recommended an experimental school run by Peace Corps veterans and based half the year in the Rockies for wilderness survival, the other half in the South Bronx, where they restored burned-out apartments. The fees were very expensive but included karate and ballet lessons.

At about this time Becky's parents began their slow falling apart; that took up almost fifteen years. It started gradually but sped up: her mother's blurred vision, her father's lost balance and swollen prostate, her mother's first heart attack, sodium-free diets, then no sugar, broken hips, walkers, commodes, wheelchairs, rubber sheets, adult-size Pampers, air spray and talcum fighting the bad smells, one weakness sliding into the rest. Some of their acres were sold off, but their savings just kept up with their decay.

"I'm just putting the loom in here until you begin painting again," Becky told her father, but she bolted it to the floor of his studio. Under the high rafters, she felt as if she were a harpist playing alone in a great cathedral.

Her parents were even more patient in illness than in health. They were interested in the cardinals at the window feeder, all-night radio talk shows, double crostics, little jokes on each other, Becky's thin gossip. As long as they could speak, they pled with her not to waste her time on them but to get back to the loom. They had become even better-behaved children than she.

When Jo came for Christmas simple survival was the goal. She was overweight, and her big breasts were scarcely hidden under layers of fleece, leather, and flannel. Her hair was a matted tangle. Becky stole only sideways glances at her. Comments about appearance were dangerous. So was any talk about college, studying, companions, families, next year, or clothes. Silence was safest, punctuated by Jo's heavy sighs and then a slammed door.

Jo's last Christmas at home featured the struggle over whether the boy who appeared suddenly with her at the bus stop could stay in her room. Her speaking was then limited to declarative sentences: "My honey stays with me."

"Not in this house," Becky said.

"We sleep in the garage, then." They did, emerging from the rumpled sleeping bag at noon, buttoning and zipping clothes, their boots clopping upstairs to Jo's bedroom, where they listened to tapes until it was time for the required dinner.

There was no discussion about college. Jo was through with education. "Crap. I'm stuffed to here." She touched her beaded Indian headband. "I'll take a bus ticket to Colorado."

There was no explanation of what lay in Colorado. Against Mozart and Bach, the loom thudded along on Becky's first dozen Spirit Bird hangings. They were exactly what a TV evangelist needed for his steel and glass cathedral. "The pure in heart fly to their Maker. You were inspired, inspired, Miss Pearce. Now you just promise me you won't make any more. I want these to be unique," he told Becky. They settled on an agreeable price.

The telephoned requests for money from Colorado were erratic. Sometimes there was silence for several weeks, then a litany of misery. Jo had bought a car to get to Denver (perhaps for a job?); it had to be insured; then it blew its pistons, then they ran out of food stamps; next they bought goats; after the goats, it was a windmill and then an abortion; later it was a drug bust and the power got shut off; finally they were splitting for the Coast, where at least it would be warm. The calls often came at one or two in the morning, so that in those seconds of finding her slippers and walking into the hall Becky could prepare her response. In the mirror at one side of the telephone she saw herself, grave over the sensible dressing robe, lifting the phone, and addressing this remote charity case.

Tension shot across the wires. Becky was an unskillful liar and would not extend unfelt tenderness. Still, she accepted this role as banker to Jo's fund-raising. The sums were relatively small, certainly never adding up to the cost of college tuition.

Carrying trays into her parents' sickrooms and changing their beds, Becky felt that she had become their mother. Sending money to Jo to repair an ancient house or to have a well dug, she felt that she was supporting a sour pioneer grandmother. Busy with the giant birds soaring in dense wool, she sometimes wove through the whole night and was puzzled by the strange light in the east until she realized that it was dawn.

One spring Jo stopped for a night, sleeping in a dented van with someone she introduced only as "my current man." He seemed not to be able to read or write, but he talked a lot. He walked lightly through Becky's house, picking up objects and reluctantly putting them down in different places. He admitted that small towns spooked him, and he asked her when she was going to get rid of the elaborate wood stoves that she had recently bought. He also let drop that he had done time at both Leavenworth and San Quentin and that he had picked up Jo when she was hitching outside of Salt Lake. He talked as if the whole country were a miniature board game, and he suggested that he would have stayed longer if he had liked small towns.

After her parents had been safely buried in the town cemetery under myrtle, with slate stones Becky had designed, she changed nothing in their house. Its shabby quality came into fashion again. Young residents of the town complimented the dining room wallpaper of hand-pressed iris and bamboo stalks. They admired the deep mirrors within chestnut frames. They were honored to live near a famous weaver. Their neat, bright children stood respectfully close to the loom watching the pattern shape, their intense faces tilted toward her. "How wonderful. How lucky," the parents murmured. "How perfect everything is."

Now in Kentucky, Jo sounded less dour but gave no information except about weather and the cost of city buses. Becky wondered what she looked like now. Would she be walking through the downtown of some tired old city in white plastic boots under a skimpy skirt and a fleece jacket, swinging a tiny shoulder purse? Would she be pushing a damp cloth over the counter and jollying up the morning's first customer, "Come on. We don't have all day. What'll it be? Bearclaw and coffee with?" She probably traveled light with a banged-up suitcase, a hair dryer, a lot of bright little scarves, and a supply of birth control pills.

Once in Instanbul, where Becky had flown to look at rugs, she had stopped for mint tea in a cafe where her nearsighted eyes mistook the waitress for Jo. The girl's big body was concealed under billowing Indian cotton and her hair was frizzed into a fuzzy halo. Up close, her face was a stranger's, but she was friendly. The cafe was filthy, and its bent tables bounced around the stone floor. The girl had settled there close to the Suleiman mosque where the muezzin allowed her to meditate at hours when there were no formal prayers.

"My feet gain truth through the layers of rugs," she told Becky. "I don't know how to say it, but, like, all this seems right. I grew up in New Jersey, which is, you know, like nowhere. So this is home."

"How do your parents feel about it?" Becky asked.

"Oh, they're far out too. Like Christian Science. But sort of lapsed now. We get on fine in different hemispheres. They send me money. I'm like a remittance person."

She was a nice girl. Becky would have liked to have given her money but left a large tip.

At last after the longest silence from Jo, six months, the telephone call about her came in a gentle voice from a small southern city. It was a staff physician at Mercy Hospital explaining that a Jo Pearce had been brought into the emergency room the day before and was now in intensive care. There had been some controversy about her next of kin.

"She's really in shocking condition," he said. "It's pneumonia now, and she's not fighting it. My guess is that it began as infectious hepatitis, exaggerated by malnourishment. They keep them underfed and force them to run around all day selling things."

"Who does?" Becky asked.

"The Sons and Daughters of the Master. It's one of those cults. They have a quota of candy and flowers to sell before they are allowed back in for the night. The waiting room here is crowded with them. They've camped out. The police suggested I call you and see what you want to do."

"I don't understand," Becky said.

"Some city employees cutting grass found your daughter unconscious in the Music Shell in Washington Park. She was probably out there for a day or so. The group didn't report her missing. They try to handle illness themselves. And when they found that she had been picked up, they tried to get her back. We found your address in her wallet."

"Have you been able to talk with her? She may not want me to come."

"It's not a matter of what she wants now. She is in guarded condition, experiencing great difficulty in breathing. We're suctioning, and she's on oxygen." His voice was sharp.

The pause that followed was too long, Becky realized. "Of course, I'll get there as soon as possible. What should I bring?"

It was his turn for silence. "She's past needing anything now. Have you seen her recently?"

"No, not in the last year." Becky was ashamed to admit it was more than three.

"Well, people change," he said lamely.

Becky thanked him for calling. For a long time she sat at the kitchen table staring at a design for a hanging she had planned to begin the next day. She lost herself for a while in the space between two bare winter trees. She was faintly conscious that she was putting off telephoning. "If I don't go, if I don't see her, it won't be true. What good can I do there?" By the time she did make the flight arrangements, she had missed the last plane for that day.

So it was late the next afternoon when, on the second leg of her flight, she landed in the old southern city, already lushly green in early spring. She took a taxi from the airport directly to the hospital along miles of dimly lighted one-family houses with small front porches, big shabby cars parked at the curb, and finally the meandering old hospital, its several additions raying out from the main Victorian structure. The taxi stopped under a portico, and the driver nodded respectfully as she shut the door.

When she had telephoned from the airport, the doctor had given her directions to the intensive care unit. Out of the corner of her eye she was aware of a waiting room crowded with several strained-looking young people who stared angrily as she passed. One followed at her shoulder straight to the entrance, which he blocked.

"You're not her real mother. Why did you come? She doesn't need you."

"Please get out of my way," Becky said. She did not want to touch him. Through his sparse and short hair his scalp looked blue. He wore a white shirt and a shiny black tie.

"She told us about you. You never gave her any love. She doesn't want to see you. She has a real family now."

Hearing their voices, a nurse within the unit came out to push him aside and to let Becky in. All around the crib-like bed were machines sucking, puffing, blinking, pulsing, humming. Jo was given over to them, her eyes only open to slits that made no contact. From her throat came gargling rasps. Her whole body was absorbed with the struggle to draw the next breath.

"Is she conscious? Does she know me?" Becky asked the nurse.

"Probably not."

"Are you sure she isn't feeling pain?"

"Discomfort, certainly. But not great pain."

"How hard it is for her. How hard it always was." Becky lifted one of Jo's hands to her lips and kissed it. The hand was like a ridged shell, light and cold. The nails were bitten down to their cushions.

Within the unit there was no space for personal possessions and no chair for sitting. Becky had brought flowers, which the nurse waved aside as she gestured her back to the waiting room.

There on the green plastic chairs were a dozen of the Sons and Daughters huddled over their Bibles, moving their fingers over the lines. Two had clasped hands and were praying, forehead to forehead. For Becky the margins of faith mattered more than the center. She liked the getting ready to go to church and the swell of the organ at the end. Out of duty to her parents, she classified herself as socially Episcopalian. She had never been tempted by the possibilities of faith.

She fled to the coffee shop, which was presided over by a comfortable woman in a rose-colored smock. "Say, you look all tuckered out, dear. It's bad enough that she's so sick, but you have to put up with them. I'm a Christian myself, but not their kind."

Becky supposed that she should be able to cry. All she could feel was fear and irritation. She wished that she was back home at the loom or feeding the cats or walking into the potting shed or even looking at the evening news. What did this strange place have to do with her? Still, it was to be gotten through until enough suffering had been exacted.

Every hour, for ten minutes, she returned to stare at Jo's tense body and to pat the sheets around her. Before midnight, at a signal from the young man who had spoken to her, the Sons and Daughters fled, scowling. None of them looked in her direction. Their empty circle of chairs remained.

At five o'clock the next morning, she awakened stiffly from the waiting-room bench. Someone had covered her with a blanket. Jo had been moved from intensive care into a private room. Becky sensed from the absent machinery that they had given up on her. Patients who do not recover are embarrassments, she realized, like children who die before their parents.

Jo's breathing was irregular and fainter, rising like feeble static. Becky struggled to think of something important to say to her, some honest blessing, but no message came. She guessed that Jo would probably resent her standing there staring with stuck tongue and twisting hands. How hard it is, she thought, to be a satisfactory human being, let alone child or parent. One succeeds by sheer luck.

Already Becky was confused about time, how long she had been there. She could not tell the function of the people who drifted in and out of the room, some in uniform, all quite relaxed.

When she came back from another nervous walk to the lounge, she found an aide bending over Jo's bed, holding one hand, blotting her face with a towel, speaking confidently as if it were really a conversation. "It's all right, Jo. Open your eyes, Jo. See, you have a visitor."

"You're very gentle," Becky said.

"I always say their names just in case they can hear. She's your sister, huh?"

"No, my daughter."

The aide glanced at Becky's face and back at Jo's. "I guess she's been through a lot. It shows."

"Yes, that's certainly true," Becky said. "In my family we were born with our completed faces. She was an old child."

"Oh, you must feel perfectly awful," the aide said and retreated, embarrassed.

It was mid-morning before Jo's breathing simply stopped. It was such an undramatic moment that Becky waited for the breathing to begin again, but it did not.

Becky waited in a small office for forms to be brought. Finally a large, competent man arrived with a business card announcing that he represented a burial society. "It's all up to you," he said. "That gang she was mixed up with couldn't care less. See, they've run out on her. At the end you can only depend on your own. I know this is rough on you. But I'd advise cremation. Gives you a little more time to figure out what you want to do. It's the modern way." He smiled gently, proud to represent a practical service.

Providently, Becky had a large balance in her checking account but was surprised at the modest cost.

Everyone in the pretty town was very kind. The memorial service was packed. After a decent interval, Becky designed a proper slate stone for Jo, who was finally safe home.

Calendar Day

No one in my family ever seemed to be comfortable in the present. Things happened too late or too early for us. Consequently, we were always playing the great scenes over in our heads several months too late. Or we wore ourselves out waiting and fell asleep before the major attraction. I should not be speaking in such elaborate plurals about my family when there is almost no one left, which increases my obsessive search to get the past settled and right so that I can pick up on my own times.

Basically, I think my family wanted to avoid being noticed. They went about this with ingrained futility while they stirred inconvenient passions from which they ran. My aunts did not marry. Aunt Meg so captivated the owner of a Chinese laundry in Hartford that he appeared one Sunday at the front door holding out an envelope which contained a marriage proposal that he had dictated to a translator and bankbooks for $75 thousand, which he wanted to turn over to her on the spot. Evidently his attachment had grown over the years while Aunt Meg brought her collars for starching. She had a thin neck, which she attempted to conceal by collars that she devised which fit inside of dresses. She wore a fresh collar every day and had a supply of several dozen. After his proposal that Sunday, she served Mr. Chin some tea, drove him to the Blue Line Bus stop, and starched her own collars.

A few years later, she received a gold watch chain from the senior partner in the firm where she was a secretary. As far as anyone knew, she had never called him by his first name, but after he died in an alcoholic retreat, his psychiatrist sent her the watch chain and a packet of torrid letters, which she burned after reading one.

Aunt Isobel became the object of attentions from the mechanic at the Esso station on Pine Street. He was a weekend trapper and a somewhat unskillful taxidermist. He was almost as silent as Mr. Chin and took to leaving bundles of odd-smelling furs at the back door. After he died in a shootout with a robber at the service station and the will was probated, Aunt Isobel was the largest beneficiary. They had never talked of anything but tuneups and oil changes.

My uncle had lovely hair and a fine voice. Lonely women would call him on the phone and after long silences hang up. Once in a restaurant a nicely dressed matron stopped at our table and asked permission to run her fingers through his hair. He was usually very patient with these admirers, but he finally had to get the police to talk with the woman who parked nightly outside the house at midnight. It was not the car so much as her moaning and whimpering that was objectionable.

At any rate they were all quite modest and ill suited for living in the times they had fallen into. Like most tightly knit families they practiced conversations like fugues. You would have to have spent several hundred hours in their company to have any idea what they meant. They never mastered clichés. Despite correcting, they would go on saying, "His heart worked itself to the bone," or "Losers will be creepers." And they had private names for everything: "Look at that big flock of Meg's birds!" Those were morning grosbeaks. They called locusts the Waterbury trees because they had first seen them from the train window as they were passing through Waterbury. There was no way to set them right. Perhaps all families are like that. I certainly have had time and patience for only one.

My mother, Sophie, was the youngest but was nearly forty when she married the most inappropriate man she could find. "It was an innocent flirtation," she continued to say. "I was only singing carols. I never expected my future to be determined by a carol sing."

My mother had taken her kindergarten class to serenade shut-ins. My father's mother was the last stop on the route, but she was too ill to listen to "Hark, the Herald Angels" sung unaccompanied by twenty six-year-olds who were thirsty and whose feet were cold. My father lived with his mother in a dark ark of a house shaded by several blue spruce and a copper beech. He had hoped that their comfortable life would go on forever, but his mother was dying and he was on the edge of a nervous breakdown. No one entered the house except some gloomy women from the homemaking service, until suddenly at the door was my mother, cheerful and wholesome, managing a flock of sparrows.

Many years later on a summer trip to Washington we stopped in Philadelphia and drove by that house, almost stopping at the front. He excitedly directed my attention: "Now. Right now. Try to look through the trees into the sun parlor on the right. That's where we met. Your mother brought all those children into that room. Tracked in snow and mud. Lined them up and made them sing their lungs out."

"Yes, that's where it all began," she said.

"Just think. I might still be living there," he said, with genuine wonder.

The house had served its principal function. The people who now lived there had given up and let the trees take over. I could only imagine the sun parlor.

So he was hooked or saved by an inappropriate match. Life had been closing in on him. He had given up his job in a furniture store to take care of his mother, who died shortly after the carol sing. After that, he never did have another full-time job. My mother supported us without seeming to. He would say that there hadn't been much going on all day in the furniture store. Probably he had been laid off for not doing anything. My parents were both frightened by reality but in complementary ways. He took his dangers nearer home. They moved to the riverside town in Connecticut where my mother had grown up, and she began teaching in the very same school she had attended. They wound up living in the same house in which she had grown up. They worked hard at making it interesting.

It was a tall house, and he didn't like heights. But she would come home in the afternoon to find him on the ridge pole, pouring tar over shingles or examining the chimney. Then he would try to improve the water pressure, and the plumber would have to be sent for.

He liked to repair his clothes. As I went upstairs to do my homework, I would hear him searching for a shirt button in his sewing basket. He collected straw baskets and learned to make them. He may have been the last man in the state to use them for marketing. Finally, I got old enough not to be bothered.

And there was his beekeeping. "I have a rival in every swarm," she would say when he leapt up in the middle of summer dinners before dessert and went after split hives. He had an old table that he would slide under the branch holding the huge bundle of runaways. He spread a white cloth over the table and put down a freshly scrubbed hive. Then he would shine a mirror at them. If that didn't work, at twilight he would finally put on his veil, light the smoker, and go right after them with a long pole. He was allergic to bee stings and suffered terribly. Finally we had more honey than we knew what to do with.

He was better at planning festivals and picnics. He spent much of the spring designing the plantings in the town park and ordering fireworks for the display on the Fourth. He kept busy. He built a sailboat from a design in the Britannica and sewed together several old sheets for it. They went out in this totally unreliable craft.

"People look more attractive on the water," she announced.

"Don't go too far," I would shout at them from the shore.

They seemed to be good company for each other. I would catch them in animated conversation when they were planting tulips or pruning roses, and they would sheepishly fall silent as if I had interrupted confidences.

We all know that there is nothing like hard times to heighten the appetite for romance. It was a great period for private domestic theatricals. We even made talk about the weather exciting. Was that because there was less news or were we still thinking of ourselves as farmers?

"Where's the almanac?" he would ask, needlessly. It lived on a hook near the sink.

"Look up the Calendar Day for August," she would say.

Calendar Days were attempts to steal a march on the future, which we hoped to control. Check the horoscope. Read the fortune on the cardboard stub that dropped from the weighing machine. Grab all the good luck that was your portion. Blow out all the birthday candles. Wish on the blown dandelion. Lower your eyes and walk outside the house until you could look at the new moon over the right shoulder and make a wish. Calendar Days were supposed to prefigure the whole next month in one convenient twenty-four-hour package.

My mother was a specialist in keeping melancholy at bay. Her cheeriness was consistent. I don't think we ever had a deeply serious conversation. She tired herself out performing and saved her best performance for us.

She worked over her stories. I suspect she cheated a little with the details, but there was always a basis in fact. In the main, her characters picked their way across boulder-strewn fields and always found modest happiness.

"My godmother Calista was a hunchback, you know, but her family was very musical. She was the one who taught me 'After the Ball.' Gave me a brand new ten-dollar bill at every birthday. She had perfect feet and hands and lovely skin." Calista's three sisters were so handsome that they had to scowl when they wanted to be left alone.

She liked to frame people before they appeared, and I must say her instincts were uncanny. She foretold exactly what childhood friends would betray me.

"There are a few simple helps for getting by," she would advise me. "You have to set your mind on being interesting. That means holding back a little something for dull days. We do live so long."

They had been married several years before my father discovered that she was at least ten years older than he, but he probably never realized that she colored her hair. She had those harmless secrets: five hundred dollars hidden under various rugs, a slice of petrified wedding cake in a fancy box, a brooch with a lock of someone's hair, photographs of herself with many strangers.

Before marriage she had taught in several different places, from New Haven to Baltimore, even one summer at a Hudson's Bay mission run by a despotic zealot who never paid his staff or fed them enough. I wonder if she liked children or teaching, but she was especially enthusiastic about what she thought would be her last students. That supposedly last class of hers were pupils in a model school, the laboratory of a teachers' college in Philadelphia. They had been selected for admission, and they were well aware that they were continually being observed.

Being a good actress and thinking her life would be permanently changed colored my mother's memory of that year. She cherished all the details. And her sad delight at the year ending must have been contagious. In the photographs her face is translucent and almost lovely. She is dressed in a serge middy-blouse costume, which sounds ridiculous for an almost middle-aged woman. She is holding hands and running with the healthy, clean children, and it must have been what she persistently called "a pretty day." You just know that a fresh breeze was blowing and that the shadows fell right on the perfect grass.

They were all stars, those brilliant children in sailor suits and smocked dresses, and I was jealous of all of them. I wasted a great deal of childhood in bitter rivalries with dogs, cats, a pony, characters in novels, and children in photographs, assuming that my mother preferred all of them to me.

I used to study the faces of those phantom children, now grown up and disappeared, especially the one who had been her favorite, Eric. I tried to imagine Eric but, not knowing any real Erics, got him mixed up with Eric the Red, bare legged and bearded, stepping from a Viking boat with shield and spear.

In one of the photographs Eric was presenting my mother with the class gift, a cream pitcher which he had personally selected at Wanamakers and which we still had well protected on the top shelf of the sideboard. It had a peculiar shape, very squat and wide, and was painted with extraordinary roosters which glowed in rust and purple, their breasts swelling in the rounding of the pitcher, their exaggerated claws extending to its base, their raised beaks meeting at the spout. It took me years to realize that it was not only terrifying but beautiful and very expensive.

Years went on, one a copy of the last. We spent a lot of time, especially in the summers, sitting around. The house was divided into zones of control. The shed, library, and cellar belonged to my father, while my mother controlled the kitchen, dining room, and side porch. The front verandah was neutral territory.

On the August morning before Eric's visit, we were sitting on the verandah waiting for the mail. I had a pen pal in Greece who wrote short letters on thin paper about making cheese from goat milk and another in Japan whose envelopes brought interesting stamps. My parents expected only the newspaper.

The telephone rang. Naturally, we had a party line but were lucky that ours was simply two rings, then silence, then two more.

My mother came rushing back importantly. "That was Eric. Calling all the way from his office. He's coming to see me."

"Coming here?" my father asked.

"Yes. He's stopping off tomorrow afternoon on his way to Boston. He wanted to give me warning."

For the next twenty-four hours we had a cleaning marathon, she beating scatter rugs, mopping floor boards, soaping down the door step. I was set to dusting window sills and polishing all the brass knobs and door pulls.

By noon of the next day we sat with studied leisure on the verandah again, my father in his steam-pressed Palm Beach suit, I in pink linen, my mother in a gray and purple silk with accordion-pleated skirt. These had been our best summer clothes for a few years.

My mother kept getting up and squinting through the screen door at the hall clock. She wouldn't wear glasses.

"Is that clock right? Is it only one o'clock?"

My father pulled out his watch and nodded.

"I'm frazzled. Completely frazzled."

"Do you realize," he asked, "that this is Calendar Day for September?"

"No," she said, "I was so distracted that I forgot entirely."

We sat primly in our wicker chairs. It was exactly three o'clock when the gray Studebaker came up the driveway. It had wooden-spoked wheels and a rumble seat. Eric was a graceful driver, pulling up carefully, idling the engine for a second before turning it off, shutting the door with an agreeable sound.

While my father and I stood respectfully on the verandah, my mother rushed toward Eric but stopped just before what might have been an embrace. They clasped hands and laughed. Eric reached back into the car and took out a large, beribboned candy box and handed it to her with a bow. They laughed again and walked arm in arm toward us. I had been briefed, of course, and did my part of the ceremony letter perfect, a slight curtsey and then a firm handshake, but I felt that Eric did not notice me at all.

The starched tea cloth over the card table was almost limp, it had waited so long. I wondered if he would notice the butterflies. The cloth had never before been used and never was again. She had allowed me to trace butterflies from a pattern book on the linen and then she embroidered them in white thread, finally washing out the sprinkles of blood from the needle pricks.

By previous agreement, my father and I left my mother alone with Eric on the verandah. Despite all the frenzied house cleaning the day before, he never stepped foot inside. Of course, there wasn't much to see beyond the dense hand-me-down furniture from Grandmother's house and the large, framed sepia photographs of the Coliseum and the Forum and the Appian Way which some Latin teacher had given us.

I sat under the tulip tree and watched Eric laughing and eating. Staring up at him behind the balustrade, I thought he was demonstrating the perfection of a star pupil. His success had been guaranteed since kindergarten.

I was summoned when he prepared to leave. He shook hands again with me, looking somewhere over my forehead.

After we had waved goodbye, we sat in the wicker chairs for a while to put a margin around the event.

"I am not going to wash up just yet," my mother said. "Eric told me the most amazing thing, you know."

"What?" My father knew he had to ask.

"He told me that he had to see me again before he got married. He told me that when he was a little boy, he was in love with me."

"Who is he marrying?" my father asked.

"Oh, some girl in Philadelphia," she said. "But he came all this way just to see me."

"Your suitor," my father said and went upstairs to change into his work clothes.

Later, when the thick wedding invitation came, it had several envelopes. I closed my eyes and ran my fingers over the raised engraving, pretending to be Helen Keller. My mother kept it as a bookmark in the Fanny Farmer Cookbook until brown dots like liver spots freckled the surface.

The Bigamist

It runs in families, womanizing, like being a bleeder or light-fingered
or lazy or curly haired or having perfect pitch. At least, that's how
Mom explained Dan Lynch. The first time I saw Dan Lynch was
through a hedge, so he was like an elf framed in green. I grew up in
Mount Bethel and must have been seeing him always from my carriage
and stroller, but I was a slow learner: took my sweet time, didn't crawl
until I walked, didn't speak until I could make sentences. Vanity and
fear of failure.

That first real time was just after V-J Day. Mr. Lynch was watering
his excuse for a lawn. I had been left in Aunt Clara's garden—eight
bitty patches of the same color zinnias, two trellises with Moonlight
Ramblers, a blue glass reflecting ball on a column in the center, flag-
stones raying out to the trellises. That garden didn't have a weed. But
there was a thin spot in the hedge where I could stare across Roosevelt
Avenue to the Lynches' house. A few years before, the bankrupt
Bleachery Company had auctioned off all the two-family company
houses. Some had been bought up by branches of the same family, and
they painted the two sides different colors which met suddenly over the
front door. Originally, all the houses had been regulation white. Having
so many children, the Lynches had bought their whole house. Their
house was run down, with a mangy lawn, a big collie named Bing,
bicycles thrown over, a crooked swing under the maple, croquet hoops
stuck here and there, a clothesline always flapping with a wash.

"They never stick to anything. They start things." Mom had them
down perfectly. They lost interest after the fast sprint.

Mrs. Lynch had been Rachel Sadinsky. She had grown up on a poultry farm outside of Mount Bethel amid a crew of noisy brothers with very long noses and stunning auburn hair. Rachel Sadinsky Lynch was a lot younger than her husband, Dan. She had been a high stepper, as they say, and two of her daughters were already drum majorettes with the local fife-and-drum corps. The house was always about to explode with kids practicing trombone or shouting at each other, the radio turned on high to National Barn Dance or Walter Damrosch or the Ebberly Brothers, and in the middle of all this Mr. Lynch coming and going in his quivery Plymouth.

He was a small man in a white shirt and bow tie, and he grew even smaller inside the car, a loose-sprung sedan that jiggled along. He was a drummer and traveled for a patent medicine distributor, selling Golden Elixir and Magic Herbal Compound at a dollar a bottle. It had been a good, steady trade. All my aunts and female cousins bought at least a bottle a week and took shot glasses of it before every meal. If they ever won the sweeps, they planned to spend a summer at Battle Creek or French Lick, taking the waters and having mud packs and colonic irrigation. You could see cases of the tonic bottles in the back of Dan Lynch's Plymouth, but it was such an honest town that he didn't bother to lock the doors. Being in the trade, he used Vitalis and After Shave himself. Aunt Clara swore that he smelled clear across the street, but the way she complained made it entirely clear that she would abandon the whole shebang, trellises and all, and run away with Dapper Dan if he had ever shown the slightest interest in her.

Instead, I was the one that got seduced, perhaps because I was more of a challenge. My photographs show me as a sour child, suffering sinus attacks, quick to tears and defeat, unwilling to join the 4-H or Rainbow. I didn't know what I was saving myself for, certainly not the Lynches.

"Come here, doll," he would say through the hedge. "Don't be afraid, sweetheart. Let me show you a cat's cradle. Look. See. You can make a big whistle out of this blade of grass. Watch me. Let me read your palm." I withdrew my hands and held them tightly under my arm pits. "She doesn't trust me," he said knowingly. "I'm flirting with her. Smitten by her charms I am."

"They should lock that man up," Mom said.

"They have, after a fashion," my father said admiringly. "And in two different towns."

Dan Lynch was a bigamist, and everybody knew. He divided his week between two households in towns forty miles apart. There were buses and trolleys that connected the towns, but Dan's quivering Plymouth bounced back and forth, three or four days in Nelson, three or four days for Mount Bethel, with maybe a day or two on the road blessedly alone. The Nelson household was the original family; the oldest child there was five years older than the eldest in Mount Bethel. The other children were sandwiched in, a couple of years apart.

As you may guess, I'm great at paving over sections of the past. After seeing Dan Lynch through the hedge, I went a lot of places and ended up back home again. I even got married right after high school but it didn't take. I was a footpress operator then and dumb enough to believe in romance. He wasn't a rotten guy—only married me to spite the girl he'd been living with. They had this big fight and he thought he'd show her. On our honeymoon I thought he had narcolepsy. After that he was back to his own true love like a shot. Then we got one of those quickie divorces. So there weren't any kids. Sometimes I'm sorry about that, but after I got over to 'Nam I figured out I ought to be glad. That was after I went to the community college and got to be a nurse, RN and all.

After Vietnam I was in a big general hospital in Buffalo. Good money but I made another what you might call romantic mistake. That's when I took up with Big Red Balzano after he'd hung up his skates. Old hockey players really fall apart. Old Red used to cry all the time over the slightest insults, even imagined ones. When he thought he'd been bad, he'd insist upon being served dinner on the floor. That I could have put up with, but I wouldn't agree to being born again. He loved baptismal services and ran around getting baptized in different states. Gave him a chance to cry and get hugged a lot. I think he probably needed a mother. When we split, he moved in with a nice old lady realtor. I saw them a couple of times driving around in her Buick, her drop earrings and aurora borealis necklace and dainty pink eyeglass frames all sparkling behind the wheel, Big Red sort of slumped up against her shoulder like an airedale.

So I came home and I moved into a trailer over in Frog Hollow and I got a job in the big new convalescent hospital in Mount Bethel, the Althea Lodge. All the rooms were sold out before they got the roof on the place. With such a dim future you'd think that being old would go out of style, but it's a booming business. The Althea Lodge has less charm than a cheap motel, but the shrewdies that own it know how to butter up the local doctors and not neglect the morticians either.

You've been in one of them—and who hasn't; you know all about such places. In the daytime there's the din of TV turned high and the PA calling somebody to the crafts room and the screamers calling out the one word they remember and the carts rattling up and down. I have the night shift, so I miss serving meals and most of the medication. What night means is dying mostly and waking up scared, but it's better than trying to pretend during the days.

I'm in halfway decent shape for forty-five. Of course, my upper arms are going, and my feet are a mess, but I lace myself into my white Hush Puppies at 8:30 every night and take off to check out the old girls. It's a rare man that lasts through—mostly priest types or sometimes a whole couple, not really whole, two leftovers, listing in opposite directions, children again.

The first night there's Dan Lynch. Chart says seventy-five. He could be older or younger. Like everything about us, there's always another version of the facts.

They put out the room lights at ten. There in the dark he was trying to figure out the voice and face. "I know you," he said. "You're Anna, grown up."

"Overgrown," I answered.

He didn't smell like an old person. And while most old people are supposed not to care about Now, he was fresh up on what was going to happen next—and that wasn't breakfast or the annual Althea Bazaar.

"You were in Vietnam. That must have been hard."

"Almost as bad as night shift here." Mostly, I avoid talking about it for the obvious reasons and also because comparatively I had it lighter than most. I could tell that Dan wasn't going to be sentimental about that.

Through that winter we used to sit in the dark, he and I, whispering about the evening news and the people we'd known, just the kind of casual talk old friends can do. Then one night he asked if I could spare a little more time.

"Sure," I said. "What can I do for you?"

"Sit down by me," he said. "Sit by me and hold my hand. I want to remember what it was like." He had nice firm hands. I wondered whose wedding ring he wore.

"I like women. That's what I miss most being here."

"There certainly are a lot of women here, Dan."

"You know what I mean. Real women. I wake up in here and wonder why. Inside, I'm the same man as always. Not any age. I feel the same."

I nodded, even in the dark.

"I suppose I'm arrogant, thinking I'm any better than all these other wrecks," he went on. "It's simply that I can't feel decayed yet. And I don't want to give in."

"I understand. I respect you for it, really," I said.

"The children have been grand, just grand. They all hung out the welcome mat, but I didn't want to test it. You know I'm a widower now."

"I didn't. I'm sorry."

"It was cancer that got Meg. And Rachel had expected to outlive me, but she died in that awful accident going to the Four Seasons Cinema, taking us to see *Tess*. She was never a good driver. I don't know what came over her, but she lost control, crossed the divider, and plowed into a car coming the other way. That's why I'm here—fractured my pelvis."

"That was a lot to happen to you."

"I never figured to survive both of them. So here I am, alone."

"Not quite. You have the children."

"Right. All my children are grand, but it's not the same. Duty. I can feel it coming out their pores. I need something else."

We had those intense little chats. Then I had to answer the lights. A lot of patients who wake up in the night suddenly think they're dying, and some of them do, of course. The others want water or to know what time it is or just to see a real, functioning face.

I began to look forward to talking with Dan. No question, he had a gentle way. He knew exactly what would flatter and raise the spirits. Then we began having cocoa on my break at two a.m. If anybody had told me a year ago that I'd be looking forward to cocoa in the kitchen of the Althea Lodge at two o'clock in the morning with a seventy-five-year-old guy, I'd have laughed my head off. But we had something going on between us.

He made the cocoa and washed up. Said he missed doing the dishes. He'd done a lot of cooking in both households, he told me.

"How was it, Dan, having two wives?"

"Wonderful," he said, shyly. "I must have been the happiest man in the state. All that love. All that self importance. I ran back and forth like a bridegroom."

"There had to have been rough spots," I insisted. "For instance, how was it when you had to tell each of them about the other one? I mean, at first?"

He handled the question theatrically. He knew that this was a big moment. Of course, he'd probably answered that question before, lots of times. But maybe he was simply overwhelmed by trying to explain it.

All night outside the Althea Lodge it had been snowing, soft unplowed drifts that the highway crews had let get ahead of them. Inside the kitchen we could hear the spitting sound of icy flakes on the windows. Dan had pushed his wheelchair to the sink and was washing our cups. He explored one carefully as if it held a secret. Later, I learned that he liked to shape anecdotes. He wanted to serve them up right.

"You never saw Meg, and she's hard to describe. I can't remember not being in love with her. She was a skinny, dependent little kid. In grade school she was always sneaking in the boys' entrance, getting me to snap on her overshoes. She spent her whole allowance then buying me candy. From the time she was fifteen she went to work in the Thread Company office to save for our getting married. She made me so happy.

"Then I started traveling a lot. When I came down here to Mount Bethel, I met Rachel Sadinsky one day when she was having an ice cream soda in the drug store. She knew I was married, but I fell in love with her. Who wouldn't have? Do you remember her splendid hair? Just like something in a story book.

"And Rachel wanted to get married. She knew about Meg and the two kids up in Nelson. Didn't like it but knew they were for keeps. And, finally then, one Christmas, I came clean with Meg. That was pretty awful. But I sort of left it up to the two women. Meg didn't give outright permission. For a long time she didn't want to talk about it. But they both came around to accepting the way it was."

"Where'd you marry Rachel?"

His face brightened at the memory. "Oh, that was easy. In those days you just drove down the Elkton with your birth certificate and your driver's license, and you had your pick of the JPs. I remember I wanted to make a bouquet for her. I saw some of those big lilies, tiger lilies they were. I stopped the car and pulled up clumps of them under the headlight beams. They were a mess, but she understood. I wasn't being cheap. It was an impulse. Understand?"

I swear we had damp eyes, the both of us. Winter can be a sad time— gives you too long to sit around and ponder. I'm not much for pondering.

Of course, it couldn't stay winter. We went through the flu season, which weeded out some of the residents. Dan and I kept on having our cocoa dates. When it was my birthday I got an assortment of spring flowers delivered at home. It was exciting enough that I didn't mind being awakened. The card with them just said, "With devotion from Dan." That's class.

"My intentions are honorable," he told me the next night. "I can't stand being unmarried. I'm courting you. You probably think it's robbing the cradle, but you're not a child exactly, no matter how I see you."

Things in my life seemed to be taking a favorable turn. My sister in Akron, who's a horoscope nut, called to tell me that since Jupiter's moving out of my third house, I should begin an interesting two-year cycle. I got a two-hundred-dollar IRS refund and asked Dan if he thought I should buy a dog or take an extension course in ventilation therapy.

Instead, he said slyly, "I have plans for us."

I thought he meant going out for a Chinese dinner. There was no reason why he couldn't leave the lodge when he wanted.

"I'm thinking of our taking a weekend in Atlantic City," he said, smug as you please. "I'm trying to dope out the arrangements. It won't cause scandal, will it?"

I was holding an armful of folded laundry, which I nearly dropped.

"Don't be scared," he said. "We're not babies. What can an old man do?"

So we rented one of those campers and went barreling down the turnpikes and pulled right into one of the casino parking lots. The crowds and the noise and the shoving inside were more than we'd bargained for. Anyway, what he wanted to do was to hire a cart and drive up and down the boardwalk, but first he wanted to get into his best suit. And I had to help him. Suddenly, after all those years around thousands of naked bodies, I turned shy. I think he understood that we'd passed over a line. To me he wasn't a patient or an old man any more but someone who lived in the real world of morning papers and secrets and an extra key to the front door.

He knew all about that in advance. He'd ferreted out the whole deal. There we were sitting in the bright April sunshine in front of the hotel. I was noticing again that he had lovely hands. He'd taken off the ring.

"Will you marry me?" he asked. "Now look at me. This is serious business. I mean it."

"I'm much obliged," I said. I have no idea where that phrase came from.

"I'm a marrier. You should know that by now," he said.

"Listen. I'll compromise. How about being engaged? We can get engaged."

That seemed to satisfy him. Worn out by all the preparations, he was having difficulty staying awake.

Talking to Trees

For almost a lifetime she scorned country things—the seductive smell of June mowing, the strident swell of hylas, the companionable warmth of a barn at milking time, the fresh breeze soughing through an aisle of maples. She fought against being her father's child.

Long ago there had been a genteel war between her parents. She had become her mother's child. Her parents were an ill-matched pair, full of good intentions, as clumsy and awkward with her as she was with them.

For her father the twentieth century had not yet arrived. He was trying to get comfortable with the nineteenth, mastering exotic skills, the sort described in old books with steel engravings—cranberry raking, dowsing, grafting, wine pressing, surveying. Years later in museum corridors she glanced at his unfulfilled dreams preserved within elaborate gilt frames, the squire and his family amid impeccable horses and prize cows under groves of fluffy trees. She always walked rapidly by the Constables and Romneys and never looked at the Currier and Ives. When she settled into a twentieth-floor apartment without a philodendron, she told her friends, "I'm rid of all that." The only nature that dared intrude was in PBS documentaries about the jungle or desert.

Of course, she was still fighting the ancient battles, her parents long gone. She remembered them young, in their central struggle. Her father had not given up easily, still thinking in his addled way that he might recruit her to old-fashioned ways. He had an ironic missionary complex. He, a fervent freethinker, practically a pantheist, had selected a pious suburban wife, who was not so much frightened by the country as indifferent to it. She continued to refer to their farm as in the boonies, out in the sticks.

"What exactly does your father do?" the girl's friends asked.

She would stall. "Well, a lot of stuff. Actually, he's between jobs." She couldn't tell them, "He collects views, knows at least a hundred cows and several horses but fewer people because the animals are more important to him. He takes care of graveyards, not for money, of course. And he worries about trees. He's part tree, I think."

He never got over the loss of the chestnuts and the dying of the elms. When, in a sudden burst of March wind, the oldest apple tree in their orchard gave up and collapsed on its side, roots exposed, thin arms tangled underneath, he sawed and planed the trunk into planks and made a picnic table. Like many of the objects he made, the table was not a success. It sloped, and its surface was porous. But he brought it back to the orchard as if the planks of the old tree felt lonely. He would insist upon drinking his morning coffee out there. No one else used the table. After a few years, he faced the inevitable and chopped the soft planks into fireplace wood. Then he made another ceremony of watching them burn with their blue and rose aureole.

She fled the sentimental scene, although she remembered the smell. Years later, in a richly furnishing drawing room of a French chateau through which she was walking with a tour group, she recognized the smell and the grain of apple wood, but she did not contradict the guide, who had called it walnut. She had her reputation to guard: she was a city person who praised technology, the wonders of computers, the speed of planes. Her kitchen gleamed with blenders and choppers.

Remembering her father's primitive habits, she shuddered. Every object he owned was stained by old sweat deep into the darkened wooden handles of shovels, hoes, and scythes. He liked their being second hand. "Just think," he marveled. "Stan Polinski used this his whole life." He was always collecting slips of ivy from public buildings and seeds of perennials from the gardens of the famous, like Emerson or Clara Barton. And he would talk about it. "Look. FDR's hollyhocks and those delphiniums I stole from Wave Hill. The Canterbury bells are from the Standish plot at Swanpoint Cemetery. It was really a favor to thin them." Cemeteries and graveyards attracted him, the more remote

and unvisited the better. "I'd like someone to return the favor to me."
He made his own ink out of pokeweed berries and wrote out lists of
important projects in an elegant hand. "Cut and trim graves at Sterling
Hill. Thin rhubarb beds. Visit the Fairfield elms."

He had special lists of what he called the treasures: the prettiest days,
the most delicate trees, the most handsome rambler, the sweetest eating
corn, the best stands of lady slippers, and the most brilliant maples
every fall. And he would talk, regardless of where he was, to things—
animals and flowers and graves and stone walls and trees—often too
loudly and sometimes even with gestures and pauses. He saw nothing
odd about these one-sided conversations. While she stood mortified, he
would whisper directly into the rust-colored ears of the oxen. "Tired,
aren't you? Not much longer now. Only to the top of the hill. Then you
can have your bran mash."

She was embarrassed that, before she went to school and knew better,
she had shared his foolishness: the funerals for the cows with proces-
sions and headstones, birthday parties for the cats, trips to see an os-
prey nest. He had read aloud from Thornton Burgess and sometimes,
carried away, would launch into Longfellow or Frost, in a booming
voice. That put her off poetry for years. She swore never to get trapped
like some summer-drenched frog in the swamp of nostalgia. Was he
really happy? Did he really prefer oxen to tractors? Why did he take a
week to repair a frost-heaved stone wall when he could have put in neat
metal posts and one electrified wire? Anyway, she made sure her high
school friends didn't run into him. She asked them to pick her up down
at the mailbox, where she waited, early for every date.

Of course, she had to go on living there as a child. That did not mean
that she had to show interest in his collection of curiosities: orioles' and
hummingbirds' nests, strangely shaped potatoes, arrowheads that still
turned up in the plowing, pressed columbine clumsily mounted, a cast-
off snake skin. He spent rainy days on his collection, fiddling with
arrangements of pine cones and milkweed pods, combining the smallest and biggest objects. He even tried to give her the shell of a box
turtle carved with someone's initial and the date—1894. That was
spooky. She left the shell on the highway so that it would be shattered
and he would see.

She was her mother's ally, plotting the earliest escape. Her mother was sure that you could tell a farmer from his walk at a half mile's distance, even before you could smell him. "Don't get stuck out here like me. You have your life before you. Don't pay any attention to him, the poor man. He's mired in the past. That's why he never amounted to anything much. He means well." Her mother had once won a prize for quince jelly, but she never made another jar. "People might get the wrong impression of me." She became successful as a factory supervisor, wore her striped uniform around the house, and traded in her car every other year.

More and more they turned away from each other, he to birds and trees, and the girl and her mother to supermarkets and movies and beauty shops.

The father continued to bring them bouquets of pussy willows and nearly perfect wild roses and bunches of violets, as if he were a child. The mother would have preferred long-stemmed American beauties or orchid corsages or boxes of chocolates, but she tried to be a good sport. As long as she could, she went along with his Sunday picnic routine. He loved picnics, had made an unsightly basket out of rushes, and took them to admire vistas and prospects he'd collected. The child, sullen, insisted upon eating her lunch in the back seat of the car.

Even in the rain, he wanted them to make an impossible pilgrimage to look at some water lilies on a remote pond, through thick brush, over swampy ground, and onto an old rowboat with mossy seats. He was devoted to old things: chairs, sleds, wagons. His shed was full of oddments: rusted scales, corn planters, curry combs, candle molds, soldering sets, old metal cracker boxes full of tackle, sinkers, lures.

He made bird houses too. They started out as replicas of recognizable buildings like Mount Vernon or the Taj Mahal but never turned out right. He hoped for wrens and blue birds and tried not to be disappointed by the sparrows that showed up. "You have to study them carefully to appreciate the variations," he said. "They're really quite attractive. You know, you'd miss the blue jays if they all disappeared." Her mother gave her patient look.

It was lucky that he didn't have enough money to tamper much with their house. He did enough damage with gates and benches. His major project was a gazebo in the back yard over which he trained a grape arbor. He hoped that the child would sit inside, listening to him read aloud, but she always tiptoed away.

She could not figure out which habits of his most irritated her. Probably the tree planting and his talking to things. More and more he went off alone, or almost alone. His black cat, Harry Truman, slept beside him on an old blanket which covered the worn front seat of the Chevy. In the back, their tops waving through the open windows, were a few young trees that he would plant. The state highway department, probably amused by his request, had given him permission to plant rows of seedlings where they might be useful. So he raised locusts, maples, ash, and butternut trees, and when the saplings reached to his waist, he organized a planting excursion. Once she had gone along; passing cars slowed, confused faces stared at them. "Pay no attention," he said. "They don't know how much fun we're having." Was he speaking to her or to the trees? She deserted and went back to hide in the car. He did not invite her along again.

Anyway, years passed. Then one day on a familiar road, driving through a green tunnel under a canopy of maples whose branches linked as if they were holding hands, she was consumed by loneliness and gratitude, too late. She rolled down the window and shouted up, "Good for you! How well you've grown!"